TI
BUSH THA

LYDIA MARY FOSTER

Books Ulster

First published by the Talbot Press, Dublin, 1931.
Second edition, the Quota Press, Belfast, 1934.

This third, annotated edition published in 2015
by Books Ulster.

ISBN 978-1-910375-11-2

FOREWORD

What makes *The Bush that Burned* worthy of reading is perhaps not so much the plot, such as it is, but—as Dr. Colin Walker points out in the Introduction to this new edition—the wonderful portrayal of Irish Presbyterian life and thinking in the latter half of the nineteenth century. Whereas histories of the church have supplied a record of major events and leading personalities, this book provides an invaluable record of the essence of Irish Presbyterianism in day to day life as experienced by regular ministers and members of their congregations. The dialogue of the 'ordinary folk' is replete with words and colourful expressions that enrich the story with a wonderful charm and humour and which the author evidently held in great affection. Indeed, one distinctly senses in her writing a wistfulness at the passing of the old ways and language. There are too a number of poignant and insightful observations on life that hint at Lydia Foster's latter years being tinged with some measure of melancholy.

The text for this edition has been taken from the second edition published by The Quota Press in 1934. A number of typographical errors in the latter have been corrected and a few footnotes, as well as a short glossary, added. Unfortunately, it was not possible to trace the current copyright holder of the original book illustrations and so these have been omitted. The artist, Alfred Edward Laws Kerr, apparently known as 'Paddy', was born in Hampshire to an Ulster father and lived on the Isle of Wight from

1959 until his death in 1980. He is buried in Binstead Cemetery, near Ryde. A copy of his will states that the bulk of his property was to pass to Mrs. Patricia Mary Kerr of The Coach House, Thornton Cross, Ryde, a building that has subsequently been converted to a holiday cottage. The publisher has nevertheless employed one of Kerr's marvellous woodcut-style images for the front cover in the hope that if ever the copyright holder did come forward he or she would forgive the liberty taken.

Derek Rowlinson

Bangor

January, 2015

CONTENTS

CONTENTS

INTRODUCTION

By Colin Walker

Seventy years ago an elderly lady sat alone Sunday by Sunday in pew 55 of Malone Presbyterian Church. She was totally deaf, and it must have been difficult for her to follow the service, but there would have been few others present who were more familiar with the traditions of Presbyterian worship. Also, most of the congregation may not have known that she was one of the most successful exponents of those traditions in the Ulster novel.

Miss Lydia Mary Foster[1] was the fourth of six children of the Rev James Foster of Newmills Presbyterian Church, Co. Tyrone. When she first joined Malone Presbyterian Church she did not attend services by herself, but sat in the gallery in the company of a brother, two sisters and a group of schoolgirl boarders. The three sisters had set up a school for girls in Belfast—the 'Ladies' Collegiate, Balmoral'—first of all in Myrtlefield Park, then at 434 Lisburn Road, and finally at 14 Maryville Park. The brother passed away in 1922, and after her sisters died in 1917 and 1918 respectively the school closed, but 'Miss Foster', as she was known, stayed on at Maryville Park, enduring the blitz in 1941 underneath the dining-room table until finally having to move to be cared for by her niece in

[1] Any student of of the writings of Lydia Foster must be indebted primarily to John T. Carson: *The Rev. James Foster of Newmills, Co. Tyrone, 1850-1890 and "the Bush that Burned" in Tyrone* (Belfast, The Presbyterian Historical Society of Ireland, 1980)

Hillsborough. She died aged seventy-six in 1943 and was buried in the churchyard of her father's church at Newmills.

It was only in her latter years of lonely idleness that Lydia Foster devoted herself to writing and she went back in imagination to the rural Presbyterianism she had known as a child. As well as many contributions to magazines such as the *Irish Presbyterian* she wrote three novels with a distinctly Presbyterian setting: *The Bush that Burned* (1931),[2] *Manse Larks* (1936),[3] a story about and for children, and *Elders' Daughters* (1942)[4] which was completed by dictation when she was already frail in health. There was also a finely illustrated collection of poems and short stories, *Tyrone among the Bushes* (1933).[5] Her books were very widely read, not only in her native province but also in Great Britain and America.

She chose the then popular Scottish 'Kailyard' style of fiction which offered a nostalgic, often sentimental picture of a pre-industrial way of life. 'Kailyard', which means 'cabbage patch', was at first a derogatory term, and for some it still is. Today this genre is often viewed as escapist, 'feel-good' literature along the lines of a Scottish version of the TV series *Lark Rise to Candleford*. Yet 'Kailyard'

---

[2] L.M. Foster, *The Bush that Burned* (Dublin: The Talbot Press, 1931)

[3] Lydia Mary Foster, *Manse Larks* (Belfast: The Quota Press, 1936)

[4] Lydia M. Foster, *Elders' Daughters* (Belfast: The Quota Press, 1942)

[5] Lydia M. Foster, *Tyrone among the Bushes*, illustrated by Alfred E. Kerr (Belfast: The Quota Press, 1933)

is an invaluable storehouse of social, religious and linguistic history.

Although Kailyard can be traced back to the popular 'village tales' of the mid-nineteenth century by writers such as George Sand, Berthold Auerbach, Gottfried Keller and Ivan Turgenev,[6] probably the best known writer of this genre was J. M. Barrie (*Auld Licht Idylls* (1888), *The Little Minister* (1891)), although he is most remembered today as the creator of *Peter Pan*. These stories were often written by ministers or former ministers, such as Ian Maclaren (Rev John Watson) whose *Beside the Bonnie brier Bush* (1894) topped the 1895 American best-seller list, and S. R. Crockett (*The Stickit Minister* (1893), *The Lilac Sun-Bonnet* (1895)).

Of course, Hollywood could not resist Kailyard. A screen adaptation of Barrie's *The Little Minister*, with John Beal and Katharine Hepburn, was filmed in California in 1934, although the Scottish setting and accents were no more authentic in that than twenty years later in the musical *Brigadoon*.

Ulster Kailyard emerged shortly after the hey-day of the genre in Scotland and was clearly much indebted to it, not least because of its Presbyterian themes and its use of the Scots vernacular.[7] The lead-

[6] Ian Campbell, *Kailyard* (Edinburgh: The Ramsay Head Press, 1981) sources it much further back in Scottish fiction, in the Eighteenth Century

[7] See Norman Vance, " 'Kailyard' stories in Ulster: Northern Stories after Carleton", in Frank Ferguson and Andrew R Holmes (eds), *Revising Robert Burns and Ulster: Literature, Religion and Politics c.1770-1920* (Dublin: Four Courts Press, 2009), pp. 148-64

ing Ulster exponent was Archibald McIlroy (1860-1915) whose *The Auld Meetin'-Hoose Green* (1898) has recently been republished.[8] As in Scotland, some Ulster Kailyard writers were Presbyterian ministers, among whom was the Rev W. R. Megaw (*Carragloon*, 1935), and others, such as Lydia Foster, Mrs E. Rentoul Esler (*A Maid of the Manse* , 1895) and Elsie R. Patton (*Cloughwater Crack*, 1929) , were daughters of the manse.

Lydia Foster's books are all semi-autobiographical and depict communities in Tyrone like Newmills that she would have known as a child. As with Barrie's *The Little Minister*, which it resembles in many ways, *The Bush that Burned* is set in the mid-nineteenth century. It follows the fortunes of a Tyrone farmer's son who goes to Belfast to study for the ministry before returning to his native county to take up a position in a rural church and eventually marry. It is a Presbyterian 'Bildungsroman' (or 'novel of education/formation') which transforms into a Presbyterian romance. There are many references to leading nineteenth-century Presbyterian figures and to controversies such as disputes over abstinence from alcohol or the use of music in church services. Like the author, the protagonist, Rev Oliver Whiteside, is both a lover of tradition and a breaker with tradition.

The Bush that Burned is essentially an historical novel of nineteenth-century Irish Presbyterianism. But what is the significance of the title? It refers, of

[8] Archibald McIlroy, *The Auld Meetin-Hoose Green*, The Ulster Scots Classics, 5 (Belfast: Ullans Press, 2011)

course, to the incident in Exodus 3-4:17 of the bush on fire but not consumed by fire, when Jehovah appeared to Moses on Mount Horeb and told him of the liberation of the people of Israel. The burning bush was used as a symbol by Christians of the Reformed (Calvinist) faith, first of all by French Huguenots in the Seventeenth Century and subsequently by Presbyterian churches worldwide. The symbol was adopted by Irish Presbyterians in the 1840s, around the time of Oliver's ordination, and it bore the motto 'Ardens sed virens' ('Burning but still alive'). At the end of the novel the incident on Mount Horeb is clearly echoed when Oliver and Hester Temple are on Slieve Donard.

Like other writers of historical fiction Lydia Foster uses historical licence and, for example, shortens the time between the 1840 Union of the Synods (undated in the narrative) and the 1859 Revival. Otherwise readers could have calculated that Oliver and Hester were in their mid-forties at the end of the story.

The settings of the novel are ones with which Lydia Foster was most familiar. 'Ballydaisy' (where Oliver becomes minister) is clearly evocative of Newmills. In Chapter Five there is a description of a visit by Oliver as a young divinity student to a girls' school in Belfast—Miss White's 'Select School for the Daughters of Gentlemen'—which is obviously based on the Fosters' school in Maryville Park, although it is doubtful that the author would wish to see the formidable disciplinarian Miss White as a portrait of any of the Misses Foster.

Like earlier Kailyard writers, Lydia Foster

tempers the nostalgia and tranquillity with affectionate mockery. Her gentle satire is often directed at thoughtless adherence to those traditions which she herself seems to hold so dear. At times the satire is difficult to detect and there will be different opinions about the degree of irony. She is looking back to people in closely-knit communities who share a devout faith that they have had to defend against persecution, yet so often they appear to have closed minds, anxious only to conserve what they have inherited in the assurance that God will protect them as they serve Him in the way he has ordained for them.

For example, psalm singing was one of the most honoured forms of the Presbyterian worship which Lydia Foster knew, but she presents the choice and singing of the psalms as often having a peculiar Ulster Presbyterian bias. At Oliver's ordination service the congregation fervently sings the second version of the metrical Psalm 124, in thanksgiving that the Presbyterian Church had survived

> all the attempts of the enemy—the Episcopalian Church—to overthrow her, because "The Lord was on her side" and "had our cause maintained".

In another story in *Tyrone among the Bushes* a congregation sings the same psalm in gratitude for having been delivered from the dreaded installation of a pipe organ.

Again at Oliver's ordination service a minister from a neighouring church, Rev Samuel McConkey, delivers the address in 'defence' of sound Presbyterian doctrine and inveighs against other, non-Presbyterian churches, that might make pretensions to teach with authority:

> The myth of "Apostolic Succession" in particular he stormed, and left its defenders weltering in their gore.

Indeed, the narrator makes it clear that Rev McConkey has not the slightest doubt of the "infallibility of the doctrines, principles or practices of the Presbyterian Church." (Of course, the doctrine of Papal Infallibility was not declared until the First Vatican Council in 1870, but the topic was widely debated long before that.)

Yet if one looks at the structure of Foster's chapters, and indeed of her novels and short stories as a whole, it is evident that irony rarely has the last word.

Lydia Foster's view of Ulster Presbyterian tradition is well summed up in her poem about a typical Ulster meeting-house. It is the church of the fictional village of 'Kildarragh', which is again reminiscent of Newmills and which is the setting for her last book, *Elders' Daughters*. The poem is probably her best known work—it is certainly the most frequently cited—and it straddles her literary career. It first appeared in 1918 under the title 'The Ulster Meeting-House'[9] and was republished in 1933

[9] Lydia M. Foster, 'The Ulster Meeting-House', *The Irish Presbyterian*, vol. 24. no.12 (1918), p. 171

in the collection *Tyrone among the Bushes*.[10] It also prefaced her final work, *Elders' Daughters*, in 1942,[11] although now with the title 'Kildarragh Meeting-House', and with some variations and an added final stanza. The author adopts the persona of an old man reminiscing about the Presbyterianism of the middle of the Nineteenth Century and touches on so many of the motifs that one can find in *The Bush that Burned*, with its satire on the fusty atmosphere, the ancient bibles, the self-righteous shunning of such prelatic desecrations as stained-glass windows or hymns, and the vehement denunciation of 'Popery'. In the short poem format the satire is less subtle than in the novel, and yet here too it is evident that in the added stanza she does not allow irony to have the last word.

Oh! for Kildarragh Meeting-house, where I sat
  when a lad,
When sight and sound and wind are gone I'll
  mind the smell it had,
And when I reach the golden gates I think the
  Heavenly air
Will have that sacred fust that laid the backs of
  Bibles bare.

Its windows were just windows made for letting
  in the light,
And whiles we looked out through them and
  thanked the Lord for sight,

[10] Foster, *Tyrone among the Bushes*, pp. 34-35

[11] Foster, *Elders' Daughters*, pp. 3-4

We saw His birds, His clouds, His trees—surely
 these things surpass
The heathen's painted images on variegated
 glass.

In God's house on Kildarragh Hill I think I see
 the man
Dared stand up in its pulpit sayin' *hymn* in place
 of *psalm*.
He'd turn to stone ere our four walls would hear
 a human lilt;
We had our faults but free we were from such
 presumptuous guilt.

Our minister—I left him last—for I may hold my
 tongue,
A man content that most his pay was hearts that
 round him clung,
His castor hat, his white cravat, his doctrine, all
 were soun',
And when he touched upon the Pope—he'd tear
 his pulpit gown!

. . . .

'Tis a brave step to Kildarragh, but it's there I be
 to rest,
For "the sands of time are sinking," and my sun
 is in the West.
And if in God's House forever my dwelling-place
 shall be,
'Twas because in His great mercy Kildarragh
 nurtured me.

CHAPTER I

THE DECISION

Trust in nothing but in Providence and your own efforts. Never separate the two. — DICKENS.

IT was a scene worthy the brush of a Millet. Two backs bent over the brown earth of a potato field that was yielding up its treasure; a robin in its new red waistcoat, alighting almost on the busy spades eager for the anticipated worm; the October sun disappearing fast behind the western hills, pursued by the frosty autumn twilight, that was creeping stealthily over hedge and field.

The last spadeful was upturned. The diggers straightened themselves, rubbed their benumbed hands, and rested on their spades. The boy gatherers threw their caps high in the air with glee at their emancipation, and hurried away carrying the last load between them, while still the diggers seemed lost in reflection over their labours.

They had digged side by side each his own rig for the past week. At a glance you saw that they were father and son.

The elder lifted his head at last and surveyed the sky. "We're just in the nick of time," he said. Although scarcely past the prime of life he was called "Old Oliver", to distinguish him from his son "Young Oliver".

But the younger seemed not to hear. Even Old Oliver, an ordinarily unobservant man, had noticed how strangely quiet Young Oliver had been during that potato digging.

"It's a brave crop after all," continued the elder, and meant this pronouncement as an expression of gratitude to the Giver of all. He cleaned his spade and looked around him meditatively.

"There'll be a dale to do this winter," he soliloquized, "drainin', an' fencin', an' ploughin'. ... It'll keep us both goin'."

At last the younger spoke.

"Father, I may as well say what I have to say now. I have tried often to tell you before, but you would pay no heed. I'm going to college this winter."

"College! Are you at that foolish talk again? Why man dear! have wit."

"I mean it this time anyway."

The young man's attitude attested to that fact. They stood facing each other, so alike, the strong features of the elder reproduced in the younger, the high forehead, the wide mouth, the grey eyes, the broad shoulders—now in the case of the older man somewhat bent.

"How would you mean to compass such a plan?" said the father derisively. "It takes a mint o' money to make a minister—an' us that can hardly make the shough build the ditch[1]—not a clod over when the rent's paid."

But the resolute figure before him stood unmoved,

---

[1] **make the shough build the ditch**: roughly equates to 'make ends meet'; see the entry for **sheugh** in James Fenton's *The Hamely Tongue: A Personal Record of Ulster-Scots in County Antrim* (Belfast: Ullans Press, 2014 - 4th Edition).

his eyes fixed on the blue Tyrone hills, that bounded the horizon, as if foreseeing the future with its difficulties, yet conscious of the power to overcome.

"Poor men's sons have become ministers before now," he said, "and I'll cost you as little as I can."

"Aw! give over," said his father. "Here, take in these two spades, till I go roun' an' spake to Amos Hill about the threshin'."

The grey eyes of the son flashed. "Keep your spade," he said, "and as for mine that's the last spade I'll handle till I come back from college," and he dashed it deep into the loose mould.

....

Oliver the elder stared at the upright rebellious spade as if mesmerized. There it stood and defied him. Argument with it was useless; appeal out of the question. A very monument of determination, it confronted him solidly in his own potato field.

Turning his head he followed furtively with his eyes the retreating figure as it vaulted the "ditch", strode across the meadow, passed between the orchard trees, and came at last to the "street" in front of the long low thatched cottage.

From the byre emerged a woman, her skirts carefully tucked up, carrying a pail of milk in each hand. Her son overtook her, seized the pails and carried them into the house.

And behold! the watcher found, to his own astonishment, that instead of angry displeasure, as he had intended, his feeling was that of admiration. He wondered at this, for he was not given to thrills. Was he dreaming? The challenging spade opposite maintained its position assuring him of the contrary.

"Well, to be sure!" he said to himself, "well, to be sure!"

He dragged the ominous implement from the ground slowly, and ponderingly turned over in his mind, as he lifted each foot heavily across the field, how he would treat the situation. There was one thing certain, he could no longer ignore it. "Never yet did he say a thing but what it came to pass," he reflected, as he replaced the two spades—the innocent and the guilty—in the shed.

He spent longer than necessary on his errand about the threshing, somewhat fearful of how to meet the crisis in the home, and also prolonged the operation of kicking the mud off his boots against the doorstep, listening the while for any snatches of conversation that might float out to him from within. But none came. Then he entered in an unnaturally unconcerned way.

The drama in the potato field had apparently not stirred the kitchen from its usual demeanour. The rebel himself sat quietly book in hand as was his wont. The mother moved about, and between the "turns" stirred the "stirabout" that puffed and spat in the three-legged pot hanging from the crane.

Did she know of what had transpired in the potato field? Her calmness in no way reassured him. On occasions when his bluster had passed, her husband felt simply a fool in Rachel's presence, as she waited patiently till he had finished, and then summed up the situation tensely and sensibly. Oliver might rant and talk, but Rachel's plan was acted upon.

She drew a small round table up to the hearth.

The glow of the peat diffused a welcome after contact with the frosty air outside. Lassie, the old collie, stretched herself luxuriously on the warm hearthstone, and when the student's hand strayed from his book to caress her, thudded her tail against the floor, intending by this signal to convey to the household she worshipped, that nothing in the world could exceed her present bliss.

Rachel placed four bowls of milk on the table together with a great dish of porridge as a centre-piece, and they drew their chairs around.

In order to persuade himself and others that nothing unusual had occurred, Oliver senior treated his supper to several remarks, forgetting that his normal habit consisted of dispatching the food quickly and silently as if a wager depended on it.

"They," he said, referring to what he was eating, which like broth in Ulster bears the dignity of the plural number, "they are just a wee notion too thick ... but anything's better nor a swinge," he added pleasantly.

Rachel took no notice.

Young Oliver's spoon seemed enchanted, as, his attention fixed abstractedly on his book, it performed its journeys unerringly.

The latch was lifted and Oliver's younger brother entered impetuously and fell heartily to his supper; unconsciously the only member of the family quite at ease.

His father began a conversation with him about school affairs.

"You're brave at your figures aren't you?"

"Middlin'," admitted Davy guardedly.

Rachel took away the empty bowls to wash. Young Oliver put his book in his pocket and went out, followed by Davy. Old Oliver stretched himself upon the settle while his wife put the place to rights. Rachel had a way of presiding over her household that even her husband recognized as queenly. She finished her sweeping, put the "besom" in its allotted place, took her knitting from the window and sat down.

"Dear! but sons is ill to deal with. Now what blethers do you think Oliver was comin' over in the field this evenin'?"

"It's not Oliver's way to talk blethers," said Oliver's mother quietly.

"Well! what else would you call goin' to college for a minister be?"

She laid down her knitting. "That would be my prayers answered."

"Your what? Why a body would think to hear you that we had an incomins, an' us slavin' from mornin' to night to pay the landlord, an' I wouldn't wondher but now they'll raise the rent on me, just because I built thon wee byre with my own two fists, after the old one tumblin' clean down on me."

"Don't I know it all," she said, "you an' me an' many's another workin' early an' late from one year's end to the other, an' all we have is our meat. Now tell me if we would have any right to keep Oliver in the same way of goin', when his heart an' mind are set on another. Shure the two boys are all we have, an' Davy can get the farm if he wants it, he has no head I doubt for anything else. But Oliver's ready for enterin' college—Mr. Birch told me that himself—he says he's well forrad with the Latin an' the Greek."

Rachel spoke of these subjects in the tone she used for all sacred things. Looking earnestly at her husband she said: "Oliver, when you have a son that instead of riotin' or worse after his hard day's work, takes an' studies, don't you think we should give him a helpin' hand to do the rest?"

"But board an' lodgin' in Belfast, woman! Do you never think of that?"

"I do, surely," said Rachel. "I have it all laid out this many's a day. I wrote to my uncle tellin' him of Oliver's longin' to enter the ministry and he said it was good news, and offered him the half of his cousin Hugh's bed. You mind the letter well enough, but you would heed nothing any of us would say. That'll be his lodgin' free. As for his meat he can take a sack of potatoes and another of meal with him—we can spare that thank God!—an' mebbe we would hear of someone goin' now an' then to Belfast that would take him an' Hugh some eggs an' butter. We must try an' make some return to my uncle, for many's the kindness he has done you an' me afore this."

"But clothes! think of them! Why at college they have to wear good shutes every day of the week!"

"Well, shure he'll be doin' nothin' that'll wear them out. He'd be a long time gettin' them covered with clabber in Belfast."

"I declare you're as determined as he is himself. I suppose you have egged him on."

A smile broke over Rachel's face that turned its usually serene expression into almost rapt beauty.

"Mebbe I have," she confessed. "Anyway I have his clothes ready again Monday week."

The door opened and the cause of the grave discussion entered. All defiance seemed to have vanished from his bearing. No one spoke, and those three so dear to one another were, for the time being, held under the spell of past memories tongue-tied.

The son knew by instinct, that as ever of old his mother had won the battle, and he merely sat and waited what he knew would come in turn—his father's approval. How he longed to help him out with it! Over him swept a wave of intense love for that toil-worn figure on the settle, while a sense of pride and admiration for his father held him in its grasp.

He had never heard his father speak of "honour", but his son knew he had lived it. He owed no man anything. He had fought the elements and wrung from his not too fertile bit of land a living for wife and weans. Whatever it might have been in his youth, since Oliver remembered, he had sought no recreation, save it were the bi-weekly paper that went its round from one farm to another. Not even to his own benefit would his father have trifled with the Sabbath Day. It could be invaded by only two things—"works of necessity or mercy." Nothing short of the aforesaid could have prevented him from worshipping God in his own seat in the Meeting-house—the only way he firmly believed to be scriptural. His word once pledged was immutable.

Rising from the settle somewhat stiffly, Old Oliver lighted the lantern, and went out to make his last round for the night; and when he returned Oliver and his mother had not exchanged a word. Both were thinking the same thoughts.

Every night there was "Worship". Old Oliver read a chapter, and offered up a prayer that was really a liturgy (word to him of anathema) for the petitions were almost unvaried, and couched in the language of the sanctuary. To speak to God of his needs and desires in natural language he would have accounted irreverent—nay, blasphemous.

"Oh! God," he prayed, "who is like unto Thee, glorious in holiness, fearful in praises, alone doing wonders ... everyone at his best is altogether vanity ... sanctify us and make us meet for Thy service. ... Amen."

They rose from their knees on the earthen floor. Davy went sleepily to bed. Rachel "raked" the fire and safeguarded a spark that would burst into flame next morning with the aid of the bellows. The two men watched her movements. That was always the signal for bed.

Suddenly the elder rose, and as if recollecting something said:

"I must sleep on this news Oliver afore we settle on anything. You sprung it too suddint."

And for the past year Oliver had been trying to force the idea on his father, until in desperation he and his mother like a pair of conspirators had at last achieved their object.

Now that it was apparently accomplished his conscience pained him. Was he wrong or right? Was it his duty to go or stay? Was it really the Voice of God that was leading him to this course, or merely earthly ambition?

"I will not go without your consent, father," he said, "and I'll help you all I can when the session's over. I'll be home again before the worst of the work begins."

"I will not keep you back, if your mind's set on it. You were aye a good son to me." It cost his father something to say anything of such an intimate nature, and he almost fled after doing so, but the son treasured those words in his heart for a lifetime.

CHAPTER II

THE DEPARTURE

Little ships must keep the shore,
Larger ships may venture more.

IT was Oliver's last night at home. He did not know that he had slept until a gentle touch on his shoulder awoke him. By the bedside stood his mother fully dressed.

"It's past four o'clock now. You'd better be risin', Oliver."

"I suppose you never closed an eye at all, mother?"

"Not a wink. There'll be plenty of time for sleep when you're gone."

"Is my father up?"

"He is. He's out givin' the mare her feed."

"What's the morning like, mother?"

"It's rainin' very weighty."

She laid the tall brass candlestick on a high chest-of-drawers, yet seemed unable to leave.

"You'll mind all I told you about your clothes, Oliver. I knit you six new pairs of socks. Be sure an' wear them time about, an' they'll do without darnin' till you're home at Christmas. An' I made you two warm shirts for when the winter sets in: I hope they'll not spoil them in the washin'; people in towns are ignorant, you know, and how they get them dried there beats me. You'll hold them yourself afore the fire to air them?"

Oliver smiled and nodded.

"How I'll miss you, mother!" She slipped away.

When he had dressed and come to the kitchen his father was half-way through his breakfast. A cresset—a high iron stand holding a rushlight—threw a faint light around. His new boots stood on the hearth. Hanging over the back of a chair was his new overcoat also warming.

His mother placed before him a plate of home-cured bacon. "Farls" of soda and wheaten bread and oatcake were on the table, and a generous plate of his mother's sweet yellow butter.

"You must try and take a hearty breakfast," she said, "for there's no knowin' when you'll get anything more." Oliver did his best, aware all the time that he was disappointing her. She never sat down, but hovered over him, his boots, his coat, his luggage.

Oliver senior rose. "It's near time we were takin' the road," he said. "I'm goin' out now to yoke the mare."

The traveller laced up his boots, while his mother stood holding his great-coat, ready to help him on with it. She swathed his neck in something—"a muffler"—she explained. "Keep it in the pocket of your coat, an' then you'll always have it," she directed.

Once Oliver would not have submitted to such indignities, but on this unprecedented occasion he was passive. Thrusting his hands in his pockets, he found both filled.

"What's this at all, mother?"

"Just a wee snack to eat on your journey."

The red painted springless cart was at the door. Rachel held a candle shaded by her hand, while the two men lifted in the small gaily-papered trunk that held Oliver's wardrobe, the sacks of meal and potatoes, and the box containing the flitch of bacon, the large meskin of butter and the carefully papered eggs. The elder man seated himself on the board across the cart, and gathered up the reins.

"Good-bye, mother," said Oliver. He stooped and kissed the cheek where the tears and rain mingled.

"Come on," shouted his father, "an' don't be keepin' the mare standin' till she gets a foundher."

Oliver freed himself gently. "Good-bye, Davy." It surprised him to find that Davy was crying too.

He climbed over the wheel and seated himself beside his father, who made a loud clicking noise with his tongue, and the mare started.

It was too dark yet to see each other's faces, and the rain and wind beat so, that they had to keep their heads down against it.

Rachel flung her skirt over her shoulders and followed, one hand on the back of the cart, as it bumped down the narrow "loanen", until it reached the open road.

"Good-bye, Oliver, God's blessing on you."

"Good-bye, mother."

His father urged the plough-horse into a jig-trot that sent them pitching up against one another in a rhythmic playful manner. Between the storm and the rain and the creaking of the cart, talk was out of the question.

The eyes of the mother followed through the darkness until the last creak had died in the distance. Then she turned and went back up the loanen very slowly.

She had made her sacrifice. Never would life be the same to her again. She paused a moment on the threshold as if afraid to face the emptiness that lay beyond. Throwing her skirt from around her shoulders she found that it was very wet. Inside the peat fire glowed red and Davy was finishing his breakfast.

She sat down to dry herself, and gazing into the red heart of the fire her thoughts flew backward. Was it almost twenty-five years since she first crossed that threshold? The home-coming had not been quite perfect. By the hearthstone sat day by day her husband's parents, helpless by age, but secure in their knowledge of the proper performance of all duties inside and out. Was it twenty-two years ago that she laid her only daughter, "Wee Maggie"—just beginning to creep—in the Meeting-house Green? And now the best loved that remained to her was gone—never to occupy the old home in the same way again, merely a resting-place till he found one of his own. Mothers' hearts were made for breaking.

Then she resolutely dried her eyes. Was she not proud to be his mother? "My Oliver," she said to herself proudly, "will never stand by and see wrong done to God or man." She thanked God for him, and rose up ready for the long day's work. Davy assisted somewhat. He foddered the cows, and carried the clamorous pigs their not too dainty breakfast.

"Of course I'll stay at home from school with you the day," he said tentatively.

"Why would you do that?"

"To keep you company."

She smiled. "Take your books an' look over your tasks, afore you go."

"I'll have to leave school soon anyway to help my father. Oliver told me to help him all I could."

"Your father will settle that. Make good use of your time while you're there."

Davy sighed heavily as he slung his homemade "satchel" across his shoulder, while his mother placed a "turf" under each arm, this being his contribution towards the heating of the building, which was accomplished by Socialistic methods.

CHAPTER III

THE ARRIVAL

Plain living and high thinking.

"YOU'RE welcome, Mr. Whiteside," said Mrs. MacBeth. His cousin Hugh had met him at the station, and piloted him to her residence in Hamilton Street.

"I hope you're not complainin'," she supplemented, for Mrs. MacBeth, whatever she may have been born, was now a professed pessimist, who knew herself to be wiser than her generation, and held the self-righteous disdain of the stupid for those who betrayed any gifts of imagination or idealism. To look on life with a cheerful eye denoted to her a sad lack of mental balance in the beholder. Her fetish was Industry, by which she meant a ceaseless performance of manual activities.

Mr. MacBeth, no doubt, contributed to intensify these characteristics, for he was invariably cheerful—nay, gay. This world was to him the best possible of all worlds, especially after being the recipient of a treat (he had rarely the wherewithal to treat himself), regular employment not being suited to his temperament. "Odd jobs", especially for Mr. Maginty who kept the spirit grocery at the corner, fully satisfied his ambitions and suffused his round red face with the halo of contentment.

Mrs. MacBeth led her new lodger to the kitchen, a place that happily did not share its mistress's idiosyncracies, for a more cheerful scene could scarcely have unfolded itself to him. The kettle sang as it hung on the "crane", while the flames in the open grate seemed to dance to its music. Two white china dogs on the mantelpiece, with those amiably complaisant expressions peculiar to the breed of the china dog, looked eternally on at all proceedings, and the brass candlesticks that kept them company seemed trying to outvie all their other shining surroundings.

"Sit down an' give yourself a shin heat, for I'm shure you have caught your death comin' in that train," she said, dusting with her apron a dustless chair, and placing it directly in front of the fire. "I never was in a train myself—it's just temptin' the Almighty to enther them—they say they're goin' at ten miles an hour!

"Here's William at last with your luggage," as her husband passed through with the sack of potatoes on his back. "Are they floundhers or skerries, Mr. Whiteside? I may say I haven't tasted a good potato since I left Mullaghadivity. These Belfast ones is that wersh they would give you the heartburn. Did you bring any meal for your stirabout?"

"Yes, some oatmeal."

"Why, but you brought some wheaten for a change? Would you think to eat an egg for your tea after your travels?"

"Yes, and boil one for my cousin too, they're in that bag. My mother packed them."

"I wouldn't wondher but they're every one broke with joultin' in the train."

Mrs. MacBeth lifted a coal with the tongs, lit a candle, and handed the candlestick to Hugh, saying, "Show Mr. Whiteside the way up the stairs, an' I'll have your teas up in a crack."

In the narrow hall there flashed on them by the candlelight a vision of fair curls, laughing eyes, rosy cheeks and white teeth.

"This is me daughter Kate comin' in at last. You'll not find her often in the house."

Kate shook hands with Oliver, and smiled good-naturedly.

"She doesn't favour me,"[2] said Mrs. MacBeth regretfully.

Oliver looked steadily at Kate, and acquiesced in her mother's statement.

"No," amplified Mrs. MacBeth, "she took clane after her father—foolish an' aisygoin'; many's the time I say it's well there's someone to take the world sayrious."

At the top of the steep little flight of stairs Hugh threw open a door. "Enter the prophet's chamber," he said.

It was a fair-sized cheerful room with two windows overlooking the street. Here was also a lively fire and a table drawn up to it. A broad bed with a gay patchwork quilt occupied a good deal of corner space.

"I see that Irish prophets don't despise comfort, anyway," remarked Oliver.

"An Irish prophet that lives under Mrs. MacBeth's

---

[2] **favour**: i.e. 'look like', 'resemble'.

government has his worries, too. 'Clothes in drawers, and books in book-cases.' That is the slogan that will be dinned into you morning, noon, and night. Here comes the oppressor of youth."

She entered with the tea-tray, and placed its acceptable contents on the table by the fire. Oliver told her how pleased he was with the room.

"Oh, aye! it's well enough just now, because I have redd it up. But if you had a seen it an hour ago, an' it's sartin you'll see it that way again—books on flure, an' books on the chairs, an' books on the very pillows you be to lay your heads on. Forbye Mr. Noble's Sunday trousers over the lookin' glass on the table!"

Hugh winked behind her back at Oliver.

"See afore you begin your tea that you take your boots off, for I'm shure your feet's soakin' in that train, an' mebbe you'll be in bed the morra or the day after."

"He'll be in it every day, Mrs. MacBeth, just as long as you let him," said Hugh.

Oliver hastened to clear his character. "I have always had to get up early," he protested.

"Well, mebbe you'll help me now with *him*. For I have a dale of steps to take in the coorse of the day, an' if I do try to save a trudgin' upstairs, shure my throat does be all the sorer belawrin' at him that it's eight o'clock when its only half-past seven every mornin'. Only for that he would never catch his classes, an' surely it'll be forgive me seein' it all goes to th' makin' of a ministher. But I'm the one knows *them,* an' when the people praises them to me, I just say—mebbe if you had the gettin' of them up in the mornin' an' the reddin' up of their books an' papers, you wouldn't waste your breath so much."

"They're a backsliding race," said Hugh.

"They're not what they were in my young days. I was rared under the Reverend McSpadden of Mullaghadivity." Paul's boast of being brought up at the feet of Gamaliel could not have been made in a more impressive manner.

"I believe I have heard of him," said Oliver.

"I'll warrant you have. He left few behind him like himself—but I'll tell you about him again, when I have time if you mind me, for I'm a bit throng the night."

When Mrs. MacBeth's carpet slippers died away on the stairs, they looked at each other and laughed.

"You'll be ready to strangle the Reverend McSpadden before many days," prophesied Hugh.

Mrs. MacBeth's substantial tea was thoroughly enjoyed, and when they had finished Hugh said:

"I'm going out to-night to a singing class. I am going to join one that is being started in connection with the new Meeting-house in York Street."

"I didn't know you were musical," said Oliver.

"I believe I am. I have a good strong voice if it was only trained, and I have one ambition and that is to shine as a singer. You can unpack till I come back, I'm sure it'll not be late."

The unpacking did not employ Oliver long. He uncorded the wall-papered trunk, and put its contents in a drawer Mrs. MacBeth had assigned him. Then taking up a book, he had got so absorbed in its contents that he did not realize how the time had flown, and was surprised when Hugh entered.

"Well, how did you get on?" asked Oliver.

"Just wait till you hear. When I went in the teacher was sitting at a desk, so I went up to him and paid my three shillings for the quarter, and he told me to go and sit among the men. There were some nice girls there, but I wasn't let near them."

"Just as well," remarked his cousin.

"When we started to sing he slipped down and listened with his ear close to me for a while. I can tell you I was on my mettle, and I sang out for all I was worth. He whispered to me to come up and speak to him when the class was over. I can tell you I was well pleased with myself, and went up as soon as the others had gone. He looked very sharply at me over his spectacles. 'There's your money,' he said, 'and don't come back again.' "

CHAPTER IV

BELFAST

Rebellion to tyrants is obedience to God.

BENJAMIN FRANKLIN.

WHAT impressed Oliver most in Belfast was not its shops nor its shipping nor yet its manufactories, but its Presbyterian importance. Here his beloved Church raised its head proudly and thrust itself continually on your notice.

Away in his corner of Tyrone it was not conspicuous. It was content simply to keep its fires warm in the hearts of men and women, who could allow Episcopacy—Prelacy they termed it, conceiving that a most damnable word—pursue its arrogant way crowned with all the honours of this world, knowing with a fixed certainty that they could await with patience their turn in the next. The music of instruments, the adorning of churches, the decking of clergy in strange garments, the genuflections in worship were no doubt agreeable to those brought up to such things, but were a poor substitute for the fact that you in your uncontaminated Meeting-house were one of the Elect.

Persecution, no doubt, had contributed to provide their minds with this satisfactory doctrine. Stories told around the turf fires of Ulster of oppression and spoliation (for Landlord and Church were synonymous terms) imbued young minds with a hatred of what these represented. Some of the old folks could boast that their forefathers in Ulster arrived in an open boat with only the "clothes on their back" fleeing from Claverhouse.[3] Life in Ulster was not exactly forfeit, but in the wider term it was denied them. For while "the Church" saw that Nonconformists did not benefit educationally or socially, the landlord or his agent enslaved them for his benefit. How well Oliver and those of a generation prior to righteous and long due "Land Bills" understood these things! As a child Oliver had wondered at the almost fury that his father could command, when talking of such matters.

One thrilling story in particular Oliver had heard his father relate with gusto a hundred or more times. Young Oliver thought it magnificent and his father a hero by reason of it.

Once, when "Old Oliver" was a much younger man, and before the advent of the ballot-box, he had actually the audacity to vote against his landlord's nominee. This enormity was very soon brought home to him by Lord Mountallen's agent whom he encountered the very next market day in Gilliestown street.

The agent immediately stopped and his attitude reminded the recalcitrant tenant of his favourite Bunyan's Apollyon, who "straddled quite over the breadth of the way".

On every favourable occasion afterwards Oliver would recount the adventure thus:

"I was sittin' in the cart when he shouts, 'Stop, Whiteside, I have something to say to you.'

---

[3] **Claverhouse**: John Graham of Claverhouse, first Viscount Dundee (1649?-1689), had the reputation of being a persecutor of the Scottish Covenanters.

" 'Very good, sir,' sez I, pullin' up the mare, an' at the sthir all the people in the market turned to look our way.

" 'Your action at the election,' he blusthered, 'has been brought to my notice, an' you'll suffer for it. Just wait till your lease is out, and I'll make you rue your d—d insolence.' An' his face was like a turkey-cock, an' he could hardly get the words out, for he ganched.

"Well, I just sat quiet till he had done, an' the scarred lookin' neighbours gathered roun' the cart an' for once in my life, I felt sittin' up there above them that I was in a pulpit.

"I looked the oul' reprobate as full in the eye as a clockin' thrush, an' says I in a voice that everybody roun' was certain to hear:

" 'Major Dunloy,' says I, 'the day my lease is out you'll have no power or ability to meddle with me or mine. On the very day that my lease is out you'll be in Hell—for you're the life of my lease!' "

This was the epic of Old Oliver's existence, and ever afterwards its narration afforded him intense gratification.

....

Presbyterianism showed him a new phase in Belfast. Large churches in important thoroughfares; rich merchants and fashionably-dressed ladies worshipping in their high pews. Men of importance in the public life of the town holding the eldership. Not so very long ago Ulster lads desiring to enter the Presbyterian ministry, had perforce to go to Glasgow or Edinburgh to attain that object. Oliver had often heard his old minister and tutor, Mr. Birch, like Ulysses, narrate his adventures. First, the seeking of a boat at Donaghadee—any sort obtainable—the voyage lasting perhaps three days if the weather proved unfavourable—the landing at Portpatrick, followed by the long trudge to Glasgow, enjoyed as only youth can.

Now, Belfast could claim a college of her own. A dignified building close to the heart of the town, bearing the name—"The Royal Academical Institution", part of which was set aside for class-rooms where professors trained students in Divinity and Arts. Seven years at that time had to go to the equipment of a Presbyterian minister. Hugh, although younger, had one session in advance of Oliver. It had not been Hugh's own desire to be a minister. Had he been free to choose, the sea would have lured him. But his mother had dedicated him to the Ministry from his birth, and he made his sacrifice uncomplainingly, for he had a gay and noble heart.

On Sundays the cousins worshipped in the new church in May Street, made famous by the oratory of Dr. Henry Cooke,[4] and filled to overflowing. They also sat at Dr. Cooke's feet in the building at the gate of which his statue now locally known as "the black man" stands.

---

[4] **Dr. Henry Cooke:** Dr Henry Cooke (1788-1868) dominated Irish Presbyterianism for much of the Nineteenth Century. An eloquent champion of orthodoxy, he campaigned against the minority dissident grouping, mainly anti-Trinitarians, who refused to subscribe to the Westminster Confession of Faith. In 1829 they broke away to form the Remonstrant Synod, which became the Non-Subscribing Presbyterian Church of Ireland. May Street Presbyterian Church, Belfast, was built in 1829 to provide a platform for his preaching. Although an opponent of the Academical Institution he lectured there in Ethics and Natural Theology in the session 1834-35. In 1876 his statue replaced the original 'black man' statue, which depicted the Earl of Belfast.

CHAPTER V

THE BOARDING SCHOOL

Journeys end in lovers meeting,
Every mother's son doth know. —SHAKESPEARE.

THE young lady boarders at Miss White's "Select School for the Daughters of Gentlemen" were carefully guarded from the ravening wolf in the shape of a young man. A cat, however, may look at a king, and the deterrent aspect of the principal, the eldest Miss White, in the pew behind her flock in May Street Church, failed to intimidate the eyes of students from glancing at poke bonnets, covering pretty heads that dare not turn in any direction save that of the high pulpit.

On returning from the prayer meeting on dark winter nights desperadoes who had probably also been devotional would have the audacity to accompany the young ladies home, and had been known to have on one occasion walked in and out through their ranks. Consequently Miss White had requested the protection of an "elder" on the perilous journey. He, good man, walked unconcernedly enough behind while Miss White would on the least alarm clutch her skirts in each hand and skip here and there agitatedly, "for all the world" as the elder told his wife when he went home, "like a hen on a hot griddle."

Also, must these precious lambs sit still until the congregation had dispersed, and they could safely trip down the steps, headed by the two tallest and flanked by the two shortest.

As they did so, an exciting thrill ran through their ranks, for by the gate stood two of those dangerous creatures from whom they were so faithfully protected. This wicked pair were our two Divinity students. The tallest young lady who led the "crocodile" smiled at Hugh and Oliver, indeed they all smiled more or less, but that tallest lady's smile was cherished by one of our students to the end of his life "and out beyond into the dream to come".

"Hester daren't even speak to a cousin in the street, or she would be expelled," said Hugh. "Would you have known her?"

"I would, of course," said Oliver, "she was a child when I saw her last; now she is a beautiful young lady."

"Is she?" said Hugh greatly amused. "To-morrow I'll take you to see her, for I have things to bring her from home. But did you notice the handsome girl with her? That's Nellie Hill—Dr. Hill of Bannerstown's daughter. I wonder how he came to have such a lively girl, for he's a pompous old thing. I met Nellie Hill one evening at Professor Wilson's, she's a bit of a ratler."

As Hugh, being her cousin and a minister's son, was accustomed to call occasionally to see Miss Temple, the maid next day invited him in, while glancing suspiciously at his companion. But Oliver was unconscious of any solecism in calling at a Ladies' School, and therefore walked boldly on. He might look a little "countrified" as yet to Miss White's young ladies, but he was well "set up", his head held back on his square shoulders, and his grey eyes fearless.

In the schoolroom the two hours' silence was in progress at which time the lessons for next day were supposed to be prepared. Seated around the two long tables, fair, red, black and brown heads were dutifully bent over *Butter's Spelling,* or *Brewer's Guide to Knowledge,* or painfully struggling with pointless sentences in *Grammaire de Grammaires,* which next day must be presented in correct French, and pursuing the vagaries of the irregular verbs of that charming language.

At the head of the table nearest the fire sat the governess Miss Lepan, reading something no doubt improving to the mind, and farthest away from her intellectual orbit usually sat Hester Temple and Nellie Hill. Every schoolgirl must have a bosom friend, and if there is disinterested friendship in this world it is in a boarding school. Alas! how soon it fades away like the morning dew! How odd to look beyond the changing years and recall a time when every thought and feeling was shared and reciprocated by one, whom if we met to-day would probably bore us by half an hour's conversation. We may grow wiser from a worldly point of view as we grow older, but do we grow more lovable? Our radiant girlhood ideals too often succumb before the sordid actualities of life and the glamour goes.

Hester Temple had only been a few weeks at Miss White's establishment, when she was summoned one afternoon to show a new pupil to her bedroom. There at once occurred an intimate exchange of information, which resulted in mutual satisfaction—

for were not both daughters of the Manse? They came downstairs, arms around each other's necks, fast friends.

The Misses White were essentially genteel, "ladylike", was the word oftenest on their lips, and absolute silence for certain periods was a feature of their discipline. Silence while dressing in the morning, silence during the hour's study before breakfast, talk being permitted at that meal—an indulgence not largely claimed since the Misses White were present. Then came prayers, after which the routine of the school began. Silence was not imposed for the long detested walk after dinner, but on return its strict observance for two hours' study was required. At tea Miss White would exert herself to test the conversational powers of her young charges, and would recite innocent little anecdotes, at which the governess never failed to laugh, but which the pupils failed to find funny.

The eldest Miss White, as befitting the principal of "a select school for the daughters of gentlemen", had ever at her feast a spectre in the form of a "young man". Waking and sleeping he haunted her. And the "young man" fully aware of this, did not give her the less anxiety on that account, but conducted himself as though a prospective Paris, who but for her incessant watchfulness might snatch away one of her fair Helens.

Eleanor Hill was practising her last piece, "Home, Sweet Home: with Variations", in the back drawing-room, when our two wolves in the shape of Oliver and Hugh bore down on Miss White's fold, and were shown into the front drawing-room, Katharine, the housemaid, hastily closing the folding-doors between to hide from the virtuous practiser this shocking view. But Nellie had had a glimpse of the visitors, and conscious of an admiring audience continued her complicated "variations". At the same time she listened for information from behind the barrier.

She heard Hester enter, greet Hugh, and then say, "Of course this is Oliver, he is not much changed," and Oliver's reply, "You have changed into a young lady, but you keep the eyes you had as a child."

Next she heard Hugh ask, "Who is making that divine music?" and Hester reply. "Nellie Hill." The music now was going *pp.*

"Couldn't you bring her in?" she heard Hugh say, and next minute Hester had pushed back the folding-doors, and stood beside the pianist, whose "variations" had never faltered.

"Won't you come and speak to Hugh and his cousin," said Hester, and the "variations" suddenly ceased and Nellie appeared in the front room.

Thus did two youths and maidens, in Miss White's very citadel, snatch a fearful joy.

Hugh did most of the talking, while Nellie at intervals looked shyly up at him, only to cast her eyes down again, and push back the curls that threatened those innocent orbs.

Hugh was giving the home news. Father and mother were as usual. Although Hester called them uncle and aunt, they were father and mother to her too, for she did not remember her own. Nancy was anxious to know if Miss Hester had put on her warm underclothing, for the days were "getting deceitful".

Also he was to tell her that Isaac was more "thrawin" than ever.

"What about Daniel McWhirter, is he back at college?" asked Hester.

"He is."

"I don't suppose he's very brilliant, but he's good as gold," championed Hester.

"He's too good to live, his pious old mother has him spoiled," said Hugh irreverently. "We had a wee joke out of them both last time he went home. Somebody slipped a pack of cards into his pocket, and when he took out his handkerchief at tea, out they came and scattered over the table. 'Oh, Daniel,' she shrieked, 'are those the bad man's things?' and then she took a weak turn. When she came to, he affirmed and protested that that was the first time he had ever set eyes on them, and offered to put them in the fire.

" 'Take the tongs, Daniel, don't touch them with your fingers,' she pleaded. So one by one he lifted them with the tongs and consigned them to eternal damnation."

"You shouldn't have done it, Hugh," said Hester, trying to look grave, but not succeeding very well.

"I didn't say I did it."

"Oh no!" said Nellie. "Indeed I couldn't believe such a thing of you."

"It's well somebody has some faith in me, for Hester has none at all."

"I know him too well," said Hester; "you'll have to keep him in order, Oliver."

"Mrs. MacBeth has already laid on me the responsibility of getting him up in the morning."

"He should have been sent to Miss White's," said Nellie, "the old bell clangs through the house at half-past six, and would wake the dead. A halfpenny fine if you're not in the schoolroom five minutes after seven o'clock, and a good hour's work done before breakfast."

"Well," said Hugh, "Mrs. MacBeth and Oliver in partnership are bad enough, but I see I might have been worse, so now I feel more resigned."

"Did you know Moses Twigg?" said Nellie. "He's from our congregation. He was far from young, and was never ten miles from his own home before, but he made up his mind he'd be a 'meenister'."

"We were all thankful for Moses," said Hugh, "he added much to the gaiety of the classes. Even the professors smiled on occasions. I remember one day he was late, and Professor Wilson asked him the reason, and he said, 'a man he knew from Bannerstown just "boorded" him at the corner'."

"You should have heard his remarks on Belfast, after his trial of it," said Nellie; "he told Papa 'there was a great "recourse" of people on the streets of Belfast'."

"We knew he wouldn't stay long; he had too many difficulties to contend with, one being his landlady who he complained 'broke her contract with him'. He had a great conceit in himself, but found that after all it was not so easy to become a 'meenister'."

Thought Hester, what would Miss White say if she heard this conversation? The very chairs looked shocked. The eye of the deceased Rev. Jeremiah White in Geneva gown and bands, from his vantage-ground above the white marble mantelpiece, seemed but to have been lifted from the volume he held in his hand, in order to administer a rebuke. The tea-bell rang.

"Oh! Hugh," exclaimed Hester, "you have stayed an hour. I'll let you out quietly."

Nellie laughingly shook hands with them, ran back to the piano after carefully closing the folding-doors, and played a few "variations" before leaving.

As our heroes crossed the hall the schoolroom door opposite opened, and Miss White's young ladies trooped out. They also shared a fearful joy. Two young men actually in Miss White's hall, and the good Hester with them!

. . . .

Tea was proceeding in the sweet silence so much desired at other times. Plates of thick bread and thin butter were diminishing fast, and cups were already nearly empty, alas! not to be refilled. It was whispered that the lady principal had an ominous aspect. Guilty consciences wondered if there were any dressing-tables left untidy, or had any young lady when out walked on her umbrella, or crossed her legs sitting in church; all these things being "unladylike", and known to cause Miss White much pain. Her rebukes usually assumed a sermon-like form, doubtless due to heredity. First she generalized, secondly, she particularized, and finally there was an application. This evening she commenced with a dissertation on the maidens of her own day. How modest, how ladylike, how reluctant to present themselves in the presence of the sterner sex. Next she adroitly proved how, by these very qualities, now apparently extinct, they rendered themselves irresistible to the creature man. "When I was a young girl," she said—and her listeners were almost sceptical that she had ever been in that stage of existence—"a Master came to the house to give us lessons in French and German, and my mother sat in the room all the time, although he was an elderly man, and the father of ten children.

"Is it strange then," she continued, "that when a young lady placed with confidence in my care, eagerly seizes an opportunity to seek the society of young men, leaves her practising of the piano, and without one word of permission enters another room to converse with two members of the opposite sex (in no wise related to her) is it strange I say that I have grave doubts and sorrowful apprehensions for the future of that young lady? The second young lady is to blame also, if in a slighter degree. She has permission to see her relative, but no other, and should have acquainted me instantly as to the other. Such a distressing incident must never happen in my establishment again."

Miss White drew down her long upper lip, drew up her lank figure to express overwhelming dignity, and returned thanks for the thick bread and thin butter (she herself had a special plateful cut on the contrary principle, flanked by an egg) and swept sorrowfully from the room.

Up the dark staircase again trooped the girls buoyantly. There is no stimulant like a scandal! Nellie Hill was the heroine of the school. So warmly was the situation discussed in the bedrooms that poor Miss White, whose nerves were in a particularly agitated state, heard the sound thereof, and her sleeplessness became aggravated. Therefore, she determined to enforce the full penalty of the law next morning.

So sphinx-like was her appearance seated at the head of the breakfast table, that no good was foreboded, and towards the end of the meal she cleared her throat.

"I desire," she said, "to say as little as possible. I have come down to the day's duties unrefreshed. When one is young sleep comes at will, but at my age, and with my load of responsibility it is far different. If only out of consideration for me you might go quietly to bed. I have found it unavailing to appeal to your kindness, and have required to issue almost nightly an order for silence by Katharine when she is removing the candles. Last night I fear it was disobeyed, and I shall be compelled to ask each young lady in turn.

"Did you speak last night after silence was given, Sophia?"

"Yes, Miss White."

"Did you, Hester?"

"Yes, Miss White."

"Eleanor?"

"Yes."

Every girl proved a delinquent. It was then only left to her to impose the statutory fine of one halfpenny.

This fund went for the support of the school library. Three neat rows of books that no one read, for Miss White was a martinet on the subject of suitable literature. The sevenpence-halfpenny added to the fourpence-half-penny already in hand, enabled her to procure *Sarah Smith; or Early Piety an Early Grave.*

CHAPTER VI

HOME

Home and the dear Home faces!
Light when the shadows fall,
Dearest of all dear places!
Hearing I heed your call.

OLIVER loved to look back on his first session at college in Belfast. Everything to the country lad had seemed magnified beyond measure, and the pride he felt in his own old Presbyterian Church knew no bounds when he contemplated its position there.

Belfast was now spreading by leaps and bounds. The prospering citizens were beginning to leave their homes above the shops and migrate towards the suburbs of York Street or Donegall Pass. Most of all he admired his own stately college standing in its meadows, with the black mountain for a background. He attended his classes with zest, and won golden opinions from the professors who discovered in him "a solid man".

Nevertheless when the session was over he was overjoyed to get home. His father met him at the end of his train journey with the red-painted cart, and the dear mother and Davy were out long before this time at the turn of the road.

It was an April day and the countryside which he knew by heart, and had so often visioned even in Belfast, seemed to welcome him back.

They passed the old familiar landmarks—the

Roman Catholic Chapel, gaunt and bare on the hill—the ancient beautiful parish Church, and dearest, although plainest of all, the old square Meeting-house where he had been baptized, and where he had heard the call to God's service, surrounded by its peaceful "green", with few headstones to tell of those who lay below. None the less were these graves treasured by faithful hearts, who looked forward to a resting place also beside the old grey walls.

Next came the cross-roads, where towered two weird giant trees. From childhood Oliver had heard the legend that a murderer lay buried here, and that these had sprung from each end of his coffin. The river, which had been a happy hunting-ground for "sprickley-begs", and where he had caught many a fine trout, swept along serenely as ever, almost reaching the sides of the low whitewashed schoolhouse, where he had begun his education, and of which the schoolmaster of his time had been highly approved because "he bate the larnin' into them". How sweetly familiar these dear sights! part and parcel of his existence for evermore.

Scenes such as these remain before the eyes of Erin's sons and daughters until sealed in death, and who knows! but these very eyes may reopen to the same sights, and find again the enchanted haunts of childhood, since "it hath not entered into the heart to conceive what God hath prepared" in the "New Earth".

At last appeared the sweetest sight of all. The dear mother watching for him. He hardly waited for his father to pull up the horse, till he was over the wheel, and his arms around her. She was furtively wiping away some happy tears, but her smile warmed his heart as of old.

And Davy, how he had grown! He would soon be able to give his father good help now. But as for himself he resolved to work hard the summer through in order to repay the debt he owed.

The old home seemed to shine a greeting in the sun. Rachel's "flower-knots" were gay with daffodils and wallflowers and cowslips. By the door was a bush of "sitherwood", a sprig of which she always placed between the leaves of her Bible on Sabbath mornings, to smell occasionally during the long service. Rachel remembered her mother carrying her Bible to "Meeting" in a red handkerchief, so prized and carefully preserved were the few volumes of that generation. Most precious of all was that Book every word of which came direct from the Throne of God!

And they were thoroughly acquainted with its contents, History, Poetry, Doctrine. So that these Ulster Presbyterians, for the most part poor in this world's goods, possessed the "Unsearchable Riches" of literature and were an educated race.

That was a happy evening. Oliver had been asked out to tea in Professors' houses, and had even handed round the cakes. But that kitchen living-room with wide chimney and glowing peat fire, and the round table drawn up to it and spread with his mother's home-made delicacies, he imagined far surpassed the town teas.

Here sat his parents whose lives had known nothing save simple living and high thinking, whose consciences were at all times responsive to Divine leading, and whose daily lives were ordered in God's sight. And these two were joyously sacrificing themselves, that they might give him what they regarded the grandest calling in the world.

"Well, mother," said Oliver, "I didn't taste butter like yours since. When what you gave me with me was done, I sometimes ate my bread dry. I was at a tea-party at a Professor's house one evening and everything was very grand, but the butter tasted like rotten fish."

"Tell me," said his father, "about the ministers. You heard grand preaching I'll be bound." His father considered that the greatest treat on this side of heaven.

"Oh, I heard just as good in the country, I wouldn't put one I heard in scholarship past our own."

"Aye, but our man's past the common," said his father proudly. "But we had a student last Sabbath Day an' dear! the conceit of him! 'What did you think of his prayers?' whispered Alick Teggart to me comin' out.

" 'I think they were a bit too flowery, an' I doubt if they ever got a yard above his head,' I told him."

"Was his name Jenkinson?"

"I believe that was his name."

Oliver laughed. "What was the sermon like?"

"'Deed, I couldn't lift half of it, for he had an accent or something."

"He's not a bad soul," said Oliver, "but a bit carried away."

"Oh, he might be a brave fellow yet, if only the Lord would give him a jag to let the wind out of him."

"Professor Wilson tried to give him one the other day. He was giving in a piece and doing it as he fancied in fine style, and when he had finished the Professor remarked, 'Remember, Mr. Jenkinson, there are only two steps up to that rostrum!' "

"Tell us," begged his mother, "about Dr. Cooke an' Dr. Morgan."

"They're both of them grand," said Oliver enthusiastically, "Dr. Cooke's tongue could wile the birds off the bushes. When he's speaking you're just carried along with him, and take his point of view although you may have held the opposite before, and will perhaps afterwards. Hugh and I go to hear him now and then, but it is Dr. Morgan[5] we sit under. See, here is his certificate," and Oliver took from his note-book a slip of paper on which was written, "This is to certify that Mr. Oliver Whiteside attended Worship regularly in Fisherwick Place during the College session now terminating. James Morgan, 7th April, 18—."

"Dr. Morgan has a splendid church, and his people are devoted to him and he is devoted to them and visits them constantly. He is called 'the model Pastor'."

"I suppose these Belfast men wear pulpit gowns?" surmised his mother.

"They do," confessed Oliver.

---

[5] **Dr. Morgan**: Dr. James Morgan (1799-1873) was born in Cookstown, County Tyrone and ordained as a minister in Carlow in 1820. He was appointed Moderator of the General Assembly in 1846. His church at Fisherwick Place was on the site of the present Assembly Buildings.

This roused his father's anger. "There's no call for them figaries. A man should go intil the pulpit the way God made him, an' not with petticoats on him. I think I see the apostle Paul in a 'gown'," said he mockingly.

Oliver thought that Paul's garments did perhaps resemble in some measure that which his father denounced, but he only said, "Well, father, Dr. Cooke would please you in one thing, he has the paraphrases cut right out of the pulpit Bible."

"D'ye mind that now!" said his father approvingly, with a knowing shake of his head.

"There's another famous man in Belfast called 'Tommy Toye'."[6]

"Surely that's not a minister!" said his mother aghast.

"He is, indeed, the best of a good man, but very odd in his ways. His church is in Great George's Street. Now, *he* doesn't wear a gown," said Oliver, turning to his father, "but he's a great smoker. One evening Hugh and I went to hear him, and he gave out the first six verses of the 98th Psalm, and disappeared. When we were finishing the sixth he returned and told us to sing to the end of the Psalm, and away he went again, because he hadn't his smoke finished. He preached most earnestly, and showed forth the way of salvation clearly, but in the middle of the sermon he came down the pulpit stairs, and poked up the fire. Then he went back again and took up the

[6] **Tommy Toye**: Rev. Toye (1801-1870) played an influential role in the 1859 Revival in Ulster. He was a smoker despite being asthmatic.

thread of his discourse where he had left it."

His father and mother looked horrified.

"His prayers," continued Oliver, "are very personal. The night we were there he prayed—'Lord bless all here present, but especially the young people in the singing gallery.' "

"Maybe indeed they needed it most," conceded his mother.

"He evidently thought so. And one evening as he was going into the Meeting-house he heard one of three youths who were standing outside say: 'Come on and let us have a rise out of Tommy Toye.' So in the first prayer he prayed, 'Lord have mercy on those three youths who came in here to have a rise out of poor Tommy Toye.' "

"And does the Presbytery not try to make him conduct himself?" said his father.

"Why he's the most respected man among them. His sole object is to save souls, and there is no doubt he is doing an outstanding work for God in his district. He knows his Bible off by heart, and can give chapter and verse for anything. Sometimes he sings hymns in his services," admitted Oliver, "and says if the congregation could afford it he would have an organ, and he holds class-meetings like the Methodists."

Old Oliver's head shook solemnly. "That man," he declared majestically, "shouldn't eat the bread of the Presbyterian Church."

"He mostly gives it away to the poor," said Oliver. "His pockets are always bulging with parcels of tea and sugar for them. He is greatly beloved, and is a well-known figure in the streets as he walks along with his eyes on the ground, and maybe two or three clay pipes up his sleeve. But if there's a sincere Christian in Belfast it is Tommy Toye."

"Oh! well if he's all that, maybe the Almighty'll forgive him his smokin' an' hymn-singin'," said his mother magnanimously.

CHAPTER VII

CHANGE

Make the most of life you may—
Life is short and wears away.

SEVEN years went by. Oliver was now a licentiate of a church that has always prided itself on the erudition of its clergy. The college tickets signed by the various professors testified to his knowledge and diligence. They also recorded that he had "conducted himself with propriety".

He had felt very lonely and deserted this past session, for Hugh always a year in advance of him had been ordained the previous summer to the oversight of Ballyswallow, a congregation not a great distance from his father's home in Co. Down. Oliver had attended the ordination, and experienced the intense pleasure of looking again on Hester Temple's sweet face. The years could never efface it from his mind's eye, nor among all those on whom he gazed daily in Belfast could he find one so fair in his judgment.

On his last evening in Belfast he sat in Mrs. MacBeth's cosy kitchen while she moved ceaselessly around doing the eternal "turns", and at the same time interjecting her decided views on any subjects that Oliver and Mr. MacBeth might be discussing, the latter meanwhile reclining at ease on the "settle", at peace with all the world. "I'm just lying here enjoyin' myself," he had said to Oliver when he came down.

Mrs. MacBeth was loath to lose the lodger who came nearer her standard than any had done hitherto. "He's that good when he's young, I don't know what he'll be when he's old," she had often declared.

Kate was absent, and her mother was lamenting her daughter's shortcomings.

"Out gallivantin' till this time o' night (the clock had just struck nine) with that dooless blether-come-skite of a MacSparran, an' there's her father won't raise his little finger."

"I'm not one bit onaisy," declared Mr. MacBeth comfortably. "If she wants him she'll not get him, for nobody ever gets the one thing they want. I didn't get the one I wanted, an' her mother didn't get the one she wanted, an' nobody gets the one they want."

"It was tellin' the one that missed *you* anyway," said his wife, "but when luck was on the road I was always in the shough."

But Mr. MacBeth was too courteous to make an unworthy retort. He merely winked pleasantly at Oliver.

Kate came in all smiles, as though the meritorious occupation she had just been engaged in assured her of an approving welcome.

Her mother turned to Oliver. "Mebbe you would give her a few words of admoneetion," she appealed.

But Oliver for once failed to oblige Mrs. MacBeth, and could only confront those dancing eyes with a sympathetic smile.

"I must go and pack," he said hastily, rising. And as he went upstairs Mr. MacBeth's placid philosophy followed him.

"There's no call to be onaisy, for nobody ever gets the one they want."

. . . .

So for the last time Oliver came back to the old homestead. How different from the first home-coming! It was Davy who met him this time. There was no one now at the turn of the road impatient to fold him in her arms. The flower-knots beside the house were overrun with weeds. Only a stray bloom here and there tried to keep the memory green of her who had loved and tended them.

For Rachel, the desire of whose life had been to see her best-loved son in a Presbyterian pulpit, was like Moses, called away when almost in sight of the promised land.

His father sat by the fireside, failing fast since Rachel's death. As of old the conversation ran on the crops and the weather, the ministerial changes in the neighbourhood, and the Union[7] of "The Synod of Ulster" and "The Secession Synod", which had been consummated: thus issuing in the era of "The Presbyterian Church in Ireland". But even as they talked, the want that existed in the familiar living-place pressed sorely on Oliver's heart. The hearthstone seemed drearily bare, and the "turf" fire appeared not to glow so red as in the dear homely evenings that had fled for ever.

It is oft-times that very one whose presence seems a very necessity of our lives—nay of our souls—who is the first to leave us swiftly and quietly. Life goes on. It has to be lived. The pitiable little duties must be

[7] **the Union**: This union took place in 1840.

performed to the weary end. We travel stumblingly on, upon a road on which the sun no longer shines, yet which by God's compensating law is hour by hour hurrying us to the morn on which "those angel faces smile".

No one mentioned Rachel's name, but all were thinking of her. To speak of her conversationally her husband would have deemed almost profane. Oliver and Davy were young, their lives lay before them, but *his* ended with Rachel's going. A restrained silence fell. Oliver said he would like a walk, and went out in the moonlight along the narrow road that led to the old Meeting-house, overwhelmed by the saddening sense of change.

The moon glorified the fields and hedges, and the little cottages glistened with an unearthly white beneath her beams. In them, too, one generation succeeded another, "swifter than a weaver's shuttle". Its pale rays softened the lines of the grey Meeting-house. Even there, no longer did Oliver's faithful friend and tutor, Mr. Birch, reason of "Righteousness, Temperance and Judgment to come", within its walls. He had also "served his day and ta'en his wages", and his pulpit was now that of another. Nature, although we arraign her changeable is in reality the only thing immutable.

Oliver climbed the low wall and stood bareheaded by Rachel's grave. He thought of her as now united to the long-lost little daughter lying by her side, and wondered had the mother found her babe "just beginning to creep", or "grown a maiden fair". Again, he thanked God for that noble mother, and renewed his vows to Him on the spot made sacred by her dust. The fears of distrust in himself that were to assail him all his life, deriding as it were, his fine moral courage, now attacked him, but as he stood in wordless prayer a wondrous calm steeped his soul, and he heard, "I will be with Thee," like a message straight from the Throne.

His father had gone to bed when he returned. Davy and he sat till late talking of farm matters. Davy, who had always longed to go out into the great world of adventure, lamented that he was now tied to the constant drudgery of the farm. His father was fit for little, and it was difficult to please him. "I'll not stay here all my life and nothing for it," he declared. Oliver could not blame him, and said so.

Davy had not long to wait, for the husband and father was laid beside Rachel before harvest time. He sold the farm and emigrated to Australia. Change upon change! They come as avalanches, and if they do not engulf us they constrain us to adjust ourselves to the inevitable, meaning "God's Will".

CHAPTER VIII

PREACHING ON TRIAL

Friendship! mysterious cement of the soul!
Sweetner of life, and solder of society.

ROBERT BLAIR. 1747.

OUR hero was now the Reverend Oliver Whiteside, and was on the "list" with five other candidates for the congregation of Ballydaisy in his own native county.

While preaching on trial there he was appointed to be the guest of William Moynagh, who had the principal shop in the little town of Innis, a mile distant from Ballydaisy. Mr. Moynagh might be designated "Mayor" of Innis, if the election to that honour depended wholly on public esteem. Other shops indeed there were, mostly public-houses, or spirit groceries, but that at which the jaunting car stopped, and bore the name Wm. Moynagh above the door, was *the* business establishment of the place, although to Oliver's eyes now accustomed to Belfast exteriors it seemed a modest enough building. There was a window on either side of the door through the dusty panes of which were discernible grocery articles in one, and in the other, ladies' boots, ladies' bonnets, and webs of different materials, intended to adorn the persons of the ladies of Innis and the neighbourhood. If Oliver's first impression was that of dreariness, it was quickly dispelled.

"Welcome to Innis!" Someone had rushed out to the street and was shaking him by the hand.

"Come in, come in."

His host steered the clerical tails successfully, so that they did not come in contact with the barrel of salt herrings that held an honourable position in the narrow passage-way betwixt the "grocery" and the "drapery", cleared a path for him through an ambush of spades and shovels, circumnavigated him past an open bag of flour, instructed him to "juke" a row of cans and buckets hanging from the ceiling, and after this adventurous voyage landed him safely in the parlour behind the shop. It was a rather small and rather shabby place, but bore that air of cosy seclusion and aloofness from the great commercial world so near to it that the race of parlours behind shops suggest. Yet it had not altogether withdrawn, but could at will hold communion with this world if desired; for there was a tiny window covered by a red curtain which if you drew aside ever so slightly revealed what was taking place beyond.

"Annie," shouted Mr. Moynagh lustily, "here's Mr. Whiteside," and Mrs. Moynagh hurried in, her face flushed from contact with the kitchen fire, and a struggle to divest herself of her apron, the perverse strings of which had knotted securely. One look at that "sonsy" face made Oliver feel at home.

"You're very welcome Mr. Whiteside, and I hope you'll feel comfortable; we haven't a very good way on us here, but I hope you'll put up with it. Here William, take Mr. Whiteside up to his room, and I'll have the tea ready the minute you come down."

As they sat at a table heaped with eatables, and in an atmosphere that almost smelt of cordiality, a load that had pressed on Oliver's heart all the day gradually lifted—the fear of the Unknown. One chapter in his life was closed, and he somewhat dreaded the turning of the page that led to another. This spontaneous gaiety, and wholehearted hospitality pulled him out of his Slough of Despond. He judged that his host was not much older than himself, but as to his hostess he was less assured, for womankind was more or less of a mystery to him. All he knew was that she looked surpassingly kind.

"I might have been as free as yourself to this day, Mr. Whiteside, only for her," said Mr. Moynagh, nodding towards his wife. "She put the 'comether' on me when I was only twenty-one years of age, an' herself hardly a day older, and we hadn't a poun' note between us when we got married. I had to borrow the cash to set me up here, and married and set up for myself inside one week."

"And you never rued it," said his wife smilingly.

"Oh, where was the good, I had just to put up with it. My nature is to make the best of everything," said Mr. Moynagh resignedly, as he pressed plum cake and honey on Oliver, and urged him to take his tea.

"Now, Mr. Whiteside," he began in a more serious mood, "I hope you'll not be disappointed with Ballydaisy if you get it. It's a poor enough place. You see most of the people round are Catholics, but you'll find them the best of neighbours if you treat them fair. There's a dale of party-work round here—Innis has a bad name—but one side's as much to blame as the other. Send in your cup, man dear? Annie, have you no tea in the teapot at all?" Mr. Moynagh seized the saucer and Oliver the cup, but the visitor had to yield on the compromise of "half a cup".

"Well," resumed his host when this contest was ended, "as for myself, I couldn't be anything but a Presbyterian, even if I was livin' in the Vatican itself. I was just thirteen when I started to serve my'prenticeship in Templeton's of Bannerstown, an' the first Sabbath Day I never thought but what I had only to dress myself and step into First Bannerstown, till the other fellahs told me that Mr. Templeton had a seat in 'Church' for all his young men, and that I be to go there. Him, the oul' renegade that should have been a black mouth himself! but married the widow that owned the shop an' turned with her. Well, I was a mischeevious thoughtless enough boy at the time, but I never knew till that minute the good Presbyterian I was! I refused to go point blank, an' the oul' bully daren't force me. I got doin' what I wanted, an' not only that but the other gomerils that had gone to 'Church' when they were bid, like weans, got valiant too an' came with me. From that day not a Presbyterian boy of us ever went to 'Church', barrin' mebbe when he wanted to see a girl, or some other fool thing."

"Away," said his wife, "and let Adam into his tea before you praise yourself any more. You'll give Mr. Whiteside a 'scunner' at you."

"Well, if you'll excuse me, Mr. Whiteside, I'll go into the shop and let Adam out, and you'll meet another of your congregation (for I know by the look of you you'll get Ballydaisy). Adam's a bit heavy-goin', but a brave fellah all the same," and Mr. Moynagh and his wife smiled at each other as at some standing joke.

When Mr. Moynagh had gone Mrs. Moynagh

said: "William can work with people nobody else would be bothered with. He gathers round him all the oddities of the town, and finds jobs for them all. Adam's the best of a good soul, you could trust him with all you had, but he's very slow. When he had served his time William was glad to keep him on account of his character."

Mr. Moynagh here reappeared with his salesman. "This is Mr. Adam Clements—Mr. Whiteside."

Oliver rose and shook Adam by the hand. "I'm very glad to meet you," he said.

Adam stood as if undecided whether he was required to make a remark or not. After a little reflection he ventured, "The weather keeps very soft."

Oliver agreed heartily. Mrs. Moynagh poured out Adam's tea, and urged him to sit down to it, and after some more reflection he decided to do so.

Mrs. Moynagh lifted the lid of the teapot, looked into it and withdrew.

"Were you brought up in Innis, Mr. Clements?" Oliver asked.

"No," said Adam, "I was not." His tone conveyed that he came from a much superior place. "I was rared in Mullaghadivity."

Mullaghadivity! Oliver's thoughts chased the familiar sound, and at last the connection came.

"Ah! I expect you were brought up under Mr. McSpadden."

"No," said Adam, "I can't say that I mind him, but I often heerd my father and mother bragging of him, an' sayin' the ministers now weren't like what he was. He had a power of big words. Few could follow him after he gave out his text. I mind my father sayin' the Revelations or Ezekiel it was all one to him, he could expound them all."

"He must have been a great man indeed," said Oliver. "My landlady, Mrs. MacBeth in Belfast, had a very high opinion of him. Maybe you knew her?"

"I did not," said Adam, "she was away before my time, but my mother couldn't thole her. She said she was aye a 'girnin' body."

"She made me very comfortable, and I stayed seven sessions with her," said Oliver.

Mrs. Moynagh and the teapot returned, followed by a roguish-faced lad.

"This is Willie," she said, "my husband's nephew who lives with us. He is an orphan, and we were lonely with no children of our own."

Willie's face shone as if it had lately had a lather of soap, and he had an air of quietude that his aunt explained was not habitual.

"Wait till you hear him whustle," said Adam (for Mullaghadivity was apparently in that district of Ulster where all the *i's* are luscious *u's*). "Oh, aye! our Wullie's the boy can whustle."

"What would you like to do till bedtime now, Mr. Whiteside? Just anything that pleases yourself," said his hostess.

Oliver said he would take a "dandher" on his own account, and Mrs. Moynagh conducted him through the narrow hall that led to the front door, rarely used except on Sundays.

He inquired of her in what direction the Meeting-house lay, and was told it was on straight up the hills from where they stood. She would have sent Willie with him but divined he would rather be alone.

On and up he went until at last he saw the small village of Ballydaisy lying peacefully in the valley below him, its gurgling river hurrying past it, eager to end its journey in Lough Neagh. He recognized the ivy-clad parish church, and further on, on a little eminence beyond the village, he beheld, where he was to preach for a lifetime—his own Meeting-house that was to be.

Plain and square it stood, the outcome of a faith that places more importance on the things of the spirit than on any earthly adornment of wood or stone.

He looked long at it. "Come ye apart," it seemed to say. That was the message it bore to the passer-by. A belt of Scotch firs behind added to its air of detachment from the world. Yet it conveyed an air of uncompromising sturdy strength that no tyranny of State or established church had been able to shake.

CHAPTER IX

THE ORDINATION

Peace be within thy walls, and prosperity within thy palaces.—
Ps. cxxii. 7.

AS William Moynagh had predicted Oliver received a "call" to Ballydaisy. Of course, it was not perfectly unanimous. Such a thing was rare amongst a race who prided themselves on freedom of judgment, and "could aye object". So there were a few scrupulous dissentients, who, having asserted their right to have opinions of their own, by and by acquiesced in the decision of the majority, and in fact became the new minister's most loyal supporters.

What an animated scene presented itself on the ordination day to that on which Oliver had first viewed Ballydaisy Meeting-house in the hushed twilight of an early spring lengthening day! Cars and gigs were heeled up along the road in front, and groups of people were dotted over the Green. Friends were greeting each other heartily, and a sense of pleasant expectation pervaded the place.

Hugh had come, according to an old compact that each would stand by the other on that momentous day of their lives. As he and Oliver walked up the path from the gate all eyes were turned towards them and conversations suspended. Strangers inquired eagerly which of them was *Him,* and were informed that it was "the sandy one", or "the lowest set of the two", although Oliver was by no means little; but Hugh possessed the power of dwarfing anyone in his company. There then ensued comparison. The Ballydaisy people professed to believe their "own man" vastly superior to his companion, but many eyes followed Hugh.

"That's the darlin' young man," said a visitor, a Miss Martha McIlroy, to her aunt, Mrs. Tuffit. "He has a face would cream tea."

"I think," said Mrs. Tuffit loyally, "that *our* man has a look more becomin' to the solemn day it is. That tall one just looks as if he came here the day to enjoy hisself."

"More than him did *that* the day, I'll be bound," said her niece lightly.

"Speak for yourself, Martha," reproved Mrs. Tuffit. "You Methodists would enjoy religion itself!"

"We don't look as dour as yous do anyway, singin' them slow psalms to the tune the old cow died of."[8]

"You should be thankful that you'll hear the Almighty praised the day in the only way acceptable to Him," said her aunt loftily. "Once (but only once)," went on Mrs. Tuffit reminiscently, "I went with your mother, who as my sister was brought up a good Presbyterian, to your wee chapel, an' we were hardly over the doorstep, when a man I never seen in my born days before, comes forrad smilin' all over like a basket of chips, an' afore I knowed what I was doin' he had shook hands with me! Thinks I to myself, you'd be a long time in a Presbyterian

---

[8] **the tune the old cow died of**: '...proverbial or slang way of describing music that is insufferably bad.' See John J. Marshall *Popular Rhymes and Sayings of Ireland*, Dungannon, 1924, Chapter III, p. 8.

House of God afore you'd meet with such behavor."

Mrs. Tuffit gave her head a superior toss, and invited her niece to follow her inside.

"Dear sen'," said Martha by way of reprisal, "that I'll be able to keep my face straight at the singin'. Have you got a harmonium yet, aunt?"

"I never was one to make a joke of wickedness," said Mrs. Tuffit. "No, God forbid there would ever be an instrument in Ballydaisy!"

The word went round the "Green" that the Rev. Silas Clegg had gone into the pulpit, and with a clatter that almost drowned the giving out of the psalm, the Meeting-house filled up.

The Rev. Silas was the latest addition to the Presbytery, and it was his duty to conduct the service preliminary to the culminating event of the day. This performance was somewhat of an ordeal, and although far from feeling at his ease, he summoned up all the volume of sound of which he was capable, and read out:

"I joyed when to the house of God
Go up, they said to me,
Jer-yu-sa-lem within thy gates,
Our feet shall standing be."

And yet it was impressive! For fervour expressed itself, and perhaps even exaggerated the Ulsterisms of phraseology in its intensity. Also, no Presbyterian can hear those words unmoved. They are their own peculiar property, the pæan of their faith.

When the Rev. Silas had finished his recitation, Peter Bell, the precentor, took charge of it from his box under the high pulpit. Peter was on his mettle to-day. Strangers from neighbouring congregations were among the audience, and would certainly "pass remarks" on the singing. He intended to show 1st Bannerstown that it had really no cause for its superior assumption in musical matters, because of newfangled ways. For instance, in 1st Bannerstown they kept rigid time, and this to Peter savoured of pure secularity, in fact seemed reminiscent of the dance. Peter's method was that he and the congregation must never happen on the same word together, and the congregation agreed with him on this matter. He kept his advance well maintained, and dexterously slid by a sort of musical ladder up or down as occasion required, if he found they were gaining on him. The congregation imitated him in a more leisurely manner, and the farther they were distant from him in the Meeting-house, the less obliged they felt to overtake him, so that while the last words of a verse were still quavering in the back seats, Peter had dashed with gusto into the opening line of the next.

It was, however, in the "old hundred and twenty-fourth" that Peter considered his triumph complete. The 124th Psalm 2nd version is still a feature of Presbyterian Ordination in Ulster. Israel—otherwise the Presbyterian Church—bursts into thanksgiving that she has survived all the attempts of the enemy—the Episcopalian Church—to overthrow her—because "The Lord was on her side" and "had our cause maintained." All the wrongs of Irish Presbyterianism surged through the words:

"Then certainly they had devoured us all,
And swallowed quick for aught that we could
deem,
Such was their rage, as we might well esteem."

Was it any wonder they applied the passionate words to their case? Ten miles from where they sang, one of their Meeting-houses had been burned down by order of the rector of the parish for daring to:

"Worship God in simple form
As Presbyterians do."

Their ministers had been fined and imprisoned. The State church had denounced as illegal marriages performed by them, and stigmatized those thus united as living in sin. Every weapon had been used against them, yet they could end their song of deliverance triumphantly:

"Even as a bird out of the fowler's snare
Escapes at length, so is our soul set free,
Rent are their nets, and thus escaped we,
Therefore our help is in the Lord's great name,
Who Heaven and Earth by His great power did
frame."

....

The Ordination Service commenced, and amid a hushed stillness, he whom they had chosen to be their minister stepped forward and knelt on the floor beneath the pulpit. Around him gathered the ministers of the Presbytery and laid their hands upon his head. The sun that had hidden behind dark clouds all morning burst forth, and shed its grandeur on the simple solemn ceremony. The venerable Josiah Hagan, with white hair streaming almost to his shoulders as had been the custom of his youth, led the ordination prayer dedicating the young man to his life work.

The prayer was very long. He approached the Almighty in a low awed voice, which gradually rose as he reminded Him of the sufferings their Church had undergone, and yet had remained faithful. He implored blessings on lands and peoples that were mere names to most of his hearers. Then he got the length of the congregation of Ballydaisy, and petitioned that they might be "inspired to hold up the hands of God's servant", and finally he came to "Thy young servant, in his high position as ambassador for Christ, that he would declare to his people faithfully the whole counsel of God so that at the last day he might have many souls for his hire. May he serve Thee, as he will wish he had done when his time of departure comes, and he goes to give in his account."

Throughout the prayer the hush was intense. No mere form of words recited. No empty ceremonial to divert the mind from the essential. No robe or stole to mark earthly rank or degree. No organ to stir the senses with voluptuous pleasure. No mysterious lights or shadows to mystify the mind. Just the greatest reality in this world as in the world to come—the approach of the soul direct to its Author. God Himself and sinful man with nothing between!

The unadorned little Meeting-house witnessed

a ceremonial that day that exceeded the pomp and circumstance of ritual as nature itself infinitely surpasses the artificial!

Searching questions were now addressed to Oliver, and he signed the Westminster Confession of Faith.

Then the strain relaxed, and a tall consequential cleric mounted the pulpit stairs. His duty was to deliver the "charge". Dr. Hill was famous for his "charge". It was considered an exceedingly fine and forcible production. Its proper designation really ran "A Charge to Minister and People". However, the former may have been impressed by its counsel, the latter never dreamt of its serious application to them. Ministers were, of course, bound to do all that it enjoined, charge or no charge—and more—for what was the good of being a Presbyterian at all if you could not find fault with the minister? Was he not your own private property and subject to your approval or displeasure, according to what your ideas on the matter were?

....

"Will you stop your fidgin' an' sit at peace," whispered Mrs. Tuffit, exasperated by her niece's ostentatious boredom.

"Could you tell me if it's near over?" asked Martha hopelessly.

"It is not, then. The defence has to come next."

"The what?"

Mrs. Tuffit turned her ample shoulders rudely on her niece, and once more fixed her eyes on the pulpit, as an exaggerated sigh from Martha fell on her ears.

The "defence" proceeded, and if anyone in the audience had ever for one moment doubted the infallibility of the doctrines, principles or practices of the Presbyterian Church, the Rev. Samuel McConkey was the man to make him ashamed of himself. The myth of "Apostolic Succession" in particular he stormed, and left its defenders weltering in their gore.

Nor did he disdain to notice various minor sects, who to do them justice forswore such abominations as "Prelacy" but were "unsound" on other subjects, such as "election", "Infant Baptism", etc. But with them his tone was rather that of pity than anger; one gathered that these misled creatures still treasured some grains of orthodoxy, which did not leave them altogether saltless.

. . . .

Out of the heavy air of the Meeting-house that had been carefully sealed up for generations from Sabbath to Sabbath, the congregation emerged at last into the intoxicating sweetness of a May afternoon, and ministers and elders sought vehicles to convey them the three miles to Bannerstown, where the ordination dinner was to be provided in McClure's Hotel. Lower mortals trudged homewards taking their pleasure in discussing the great day's event.

"It's a pity it come at such a throng season," said Archie Kilpatrick to old Ephraim Weir, "but of course it's only once in a lifetime, as you may say, an' worth a lost day."

"I suppose you hardly mind the last one in Ballydaisy," replied Ephraim—"five an' forty years ago come Holl'eve—but I mind it better than what happened the day. It was kep' up till at last we couldn't see each other's faces in the Meeting-house, an' we stumbled out in the dark. Ah! them was the great times! As the Bible says, 'there were giants in those days.' And to think that my dear Mr. Brown that was ordained that day, so young, an' so tall, an' so straight, should be lyin' in the Green, an' me left pechin' up this hill. That young man that was ordained the day is well countenanced an' well set-up. I have no fault to find with him or his doctrine the day he preached on trial, but he'll never be Mr. Brown—no there'll never be nobody like him again. ... I was the first pair he married in Ballydaisy, an' in them days the minister used to kiss the bride afther it was over. An' always when Mr. Brown done that he would say: 'This is a privilege I have, but I only exercise it on the handsome ones.' An' if they were as yalla as the duck's foot, or skellied, or was humpty-backed, he would always say the same thing. For he was that knowledgeable that he had the very gumption of Solomon."

"The Church people got it the day anyway," said Archie gleefully. "I didn't grudge losin' me day when the Rev. McConkey was reddin' *them* up. For all I couldn't folly him altogether, yet I knew he had the rights of it."

"Aye," heartily agreed Ephraim, "them that's born Presbyterians couldn't be too thankful. All their proceedin's is 'according to the law and to the testimony'. A bishop an' a presbyter's one an' the same thing. Episcopals give no heed to the Apostle Paul, but folly their own vanities 'a law unto themselves'. It's a fearsome thing to praise the Almighty with man-made hymns, made by sinful men an' instruments of worldly music. ... I for one wouldn't like to have to answer for it!"

"Neither would I," agreed Archie virtuously. "I seen Martha McIlroy there the day. She's a Methody. Let *her* take what *she* got!

"They're Armenians," said Ephraim.

"Are they?" said Archie, guessing from Ephraim's tone that that must be something bad.

"Saved one day an' lost the next! That's *their* doctrine."

"Man oh! that's the quarest doctrine I ever heerd of."

"They didn't get that from the Apostle Paul either."

"Well, I'm not sorry I lost me day anyways," Archie said by way of parting.

"There'll be days when we're dead," said old Ephraim.

CHAPTER X

THE ORDINATION DINNER

Your old men shall dream dreams, your young men shall see visions. — JOEL ii. 28.

THE Presbytery was hungry, and enjoyed its dinner. The newly-ordained minister sat at the right hand of the moderator — who was an old man with a brown wig and a very red nose and flabby cheeks. His neck was swathed in a white neck-cloth up to his ears, whereas Oliver and all the younger men wore the large white starched "cravat".

He was a kindly man, and noticed that the new minister was making a brave but unsuccessful attempt to diminish his plate of roast beef, and he felt sorry for him.

"Why, man, you're making no headway at all," he said, "and it's not for the want of teeth."

"No, it's not that," replied Oliver smilingly.

"Well," said his friend, "I'm like the old priest who said, 'When I had teeth I had no beef, and now that I have beef I have no teeth.' "

Oliver was sensible of the efforts the old man was making to dispel a depression that was evidently apparent.

"That was a pretty accurate philosophy of life," he replied.

"But man dear! your wine-glass is empty, you'll feel better when you get a drop of spirits," said the moderator.

"No, thank you all the same, Mr. Hegan, but I'm a teetotaller."

"Well, well! I've heard of those new-fashioned folk, but I haven't met many of them. Dr. Hill and one or two others of the Presbytery have those queer views. Dr. Edgar[9] of Belfast started them I believe. Now, you look as sensible a fellow as ever I set my eyes on. What'll you do at baptisms and funerals and days you go visiting in Ballydaisy? It'll be dead against you, Mr. Whiteside. Take the advice of an old man and drop these notions. We ministers can't afford any peculiarity."

Oliver did not reply. He looked down the table and saw flushed faces and heard voices becoming louder as the dinner advanced. Then a knocking on the table brought instantaneous silence. The moderator had announced the toast of the newly-ordained minister.

Oliver, as if in a dream, found himself on his feet. His speech had been carefully prepared, but alas! it had vanished, and he stood a few seconds that seemed to him hours desperately pursuing its shadow, and instead a vivid picture took possession of his mind.

It was a Sabbath afternoon in his old home. His mother's busy hands lay quiet in her lap as she read her Bible in the little parlour where she liked to sit on that sacred day. He saw every detail of the room, the corner-cupboard that contained her good

---

[9] **Dr. Edgar**: Dr. John Edgar (1798–1866) co-founded the Ulster Temperance Movement in 1829 when he was Minister of a Presbyterian Church in Alfred Place, Belfast.

set of china, the round table with its much-prized books, chiefly prizes that Oliver and Davy had got at Sunday School, the sampler embroidered with the alphabet and decorated with strange stiff trees and flowers and recording that "Rachel Noble, aged twelve years, finished this work, 18—," and underneath the lines:

"Jesus permit this work to stand,
As the first effort of an infant's hand,
And as her fingers on the sampler move,
Engage her tender heart to seek Thy love.
With Thy dear children may she have a part
And write Thy name Thyself upon her heart."

His father also sat book in hand, but he after his week's work in the open air had fallen asleep over it. Most likely it was *The Pilgrim's Progress,* which he ranked only second to the "Book of Books" itself. Davy, too, sat by the window supposed to be wrestling with his question in the Shorter Catechism for next Sabbath's Sunday School, but instead gazing enviously at Rover frolicking in the hag-yard, and beyond Rover to the trees, and the small river productive of such pleasure on weekdays, but "out of bounds" on the Sabbath. Such a picture of Sabbath stillness! only broken by the tick of the tall old "grandfather" beside the fireplace. Everything that could possibly be done on the day before ensured the proper observance of God's holy day. All the water needed carried in, the kitchen corner filled with "turf", and the door shut against the outside visiting world.

His mother turned a page, and as she did so, her deep calm eyes were raised and rested on him with that look of divine motherhood that he always saw in them. The spell was broken. Words came to him, simple enough words but honest. He spoke of his humble home, glorified alone by a constant sense of God's Presence, of his mother's desires and prayer and sacrifices gladly undertaken that he should become a minister, of her noble influence on his boyish life and character. Of the difficulties all overcome as he had been led by an Unseen Hand into the position in which he found himself that day. That he staked his future on the "hitherto", and entered humbly on his life-work throwing himself on God's guidance and help. "I purpose," he concluded, "in the strength of my Lord and Master to embrace every opportunity of preaching with the utmost plainness, faithfulness and affection, the glorious Gospel of the Everlasting God." It was not a very erudite oration, just a simple confession of faith, prompted by unseen forces. But it came from the heart, and for this reason touched the heart.

Afterwards Hugh came and sat near him, and he felt as always happier for Hugh's near presence. Other toasts were proposed and responded to in a more or less humorous manner. The proceedings ended pleasantly. Everyone welcomed him warmly and wished him success.

Twilight had already fallen, as Hugh and he believing they were quite the last to leave, went to the hotel yard to find their car. A low croydon seemed also awaiting someone. Towards it advanced two men attempting to make it appear that the figure they held up between them moved by the aid of its own feet, and thus maintained the dignity due to its sacred office.

"Give him a heave from behind while I give him a hoist up in the front. Studdy now! That's it! He's safe enough if you keep your arm roun' him an' not let him cowp over the wheel."

Oliver caught a glimpse of a brown wig awry, a voluminous neck-cloth in a state of derangement, and an inert mass on the front seat of the croydon.

It was his kindly old friend, the moderator!

CHAPTER XI

THE MANSE

A Cottage of Gentility. — SOUTHEY

THE scent of hawthorn never came to the Rev. Oliver Whiteside without bringing in its train, to a heart often depressed and discouraged, the pure joy and adventure of that May evening when he walked up from Innis to take possession of his own home. The gentle caressing May rain that had fallen all afternoon had cleansed the dusty world, and left behind it in the air the fragrance of its ministrations. Behind the hedges in the deep grass the corn-crakes had already begun their revels which were intended to be prolonged the glorious night through.

Something in Oliver's step would have told you that this short journey was momentous. He was actually going to a house of his own, which in all probability he would inhabit until called forth to his eternal home.

Almost a week had passed since his ordination, during which the Moynaghs not only held him a glad guest but helped him in the preparation of his Manse. For its future occupant the modest little place held lifelong charms, not the least of which was the sight of the white wooden gate that came on you so unexpectedly at the turn of the road. Although the building stood with its side only separated from the common road a few yards, this gate was so placed that a little winding avenue led up to the front door, betokening that it was a gentleman's place, and therefore should not be too easy of approach.

He closed the gate carefully, for he was now a responsible householder, and as he walked up the path feasted his eyes on this ordained home. It was a long low cottage with a wide green door and brass knocker, and three windows on either side. Although it was before the general era of Manses, it bore that name, and looked to him a seasoned Ministerial dwelling. He imagined it had an educated look, and an air of refined retirement, that distinguished it from the other cottages of the neighbourhood.

Forty-four years previously his predecessor, Mr. Brown, had built it for himself when in his breast hopes ran high, and life looked to him an opening Paradise. Every stone of it was laid for *her.* Through the window panes he saw her face watching for him, from that wide side window that looked out to the west. With his own hands he laid out the grounds, and in the most sheltered corner fashioned a summer-house, where while she sewed the roses would nod to her. Her favourite flowers were planted in the garden-beds. Above all she loved the perfume of white jasmine. He placed it by the parlour window.

And she never came except in dreams! Year after year the sweet jasmine sent its fragrance into the room where he sat pondering over a book, instead of Greek characters he would see a fair face surrounded by golden curls. At this vision he would close the volume, and walk in his garden for a while till the bitterness passed. Rumour reached him of her unhappiness, and that was the persistent sorrow of his life. His home he bequeathed for a Manse to the congregation whom after her he had loved best.

All these things which he had already heard, Oliver called to mind as he looked at the tastefully laid out little grounds, which seemed to preach a sermon to him on the text, "Love is stronger than Death."

....

He was, however, distracted from the old minister's romance by the sudden opening of the green door, by Ann Moriarty, whom Mrs. Moynagh had appointed to be his housekeeper, failing any more capable applicant. Ann looked of that age that is supposed to bring wisdom in its train, but in her case a cunning simplicity was the nearest approach to that faculty. Her foolish wide mouth was stretched to its utmost in greeting.

"Your Reverence is entirely welcome, an' may you live till you die in this purty place."

He stepped in a very happy frame of mind into the little square hall which a window made cheerful.

"I'm just makin' the stirabout for Your Reverence's supper that Mrs. Moynagh warned me never to miss. Would you care to take a shin hate of the kitchen fire afther yer walk?"

Oliver felt quite warm but followed Ann agreeably into her domain where a little black three-legged pot hung on a crane over the "turf" fire, the contents of which bubbled and jumped in a joyous frenzy of furious boiling.

"Does Your Reverence like them thick?"

"Middling," said Oliver cautiously.

"That's just the way I like them myself, so you an' me'll agree."

He looked with pleasure at the dresser which Mrs. Moynagh had furnished with blue willow dishes and plates, and admired them audibly.

"We be to watch ourselves han'lin' them," said Ann with a tone of partnership, and a knowing little shake of her head, that made their owner turn away to hide a smile.

From room to room he passed in almost childish excitement. The barest necessities of furniture only had place. The parlour to the right of the hall had two bedrooms opening off it, and his own contained a richly carved four-poster that Mrs. Moynagh had bought at Lady Elizabeth Carden's auction, and in the parlour were Chippendale chairs and a gate-legged table also obtained there which she considered terribly out of date, but would do the minister's requirements till he could afford more modern fashionable articles.

He recrossed the flagged hall and wandered into the other side of the house. Here was her drawing-room which for forty-five years had remained unoccupied; save as a library to house the old minister's books. Opening out of it were also two bedrooms. It was quite a pleasant little walk from one end of the cottage to the other, but Oliver was interrupted by Ann announcing:

"I have emptied your stirabout on the parlour table, mebbe it'll be a wee bit swinged with the talkin' of Yer Reverence, but it'll be all the wholesomer for that."

She led the way to the parlour, and stood in a

conversational attitude. "You'd betther let them cool awhile."

Her master was a little embarrassed as to how to address a female so far in years beyond his own.

"I forgot to ask Mrs. Moynagh if you were married, and do not know whether I should call you 'Mrs.' or not," he said.

"I nivver was married nor nivver was axed," said Ann candidly, "but shure we must just be content with our lot not but what I hope it won't be Yer Riverence's. How many eggs would you propose to ate for your breakfast?"

"One please."

"Well, I'll bid Yer Riverence a good night, and may the saints sen' you soun' sleep!"

There was no doubt the porridge was "swinged", but Oliver urged himself to eat a respectable portion, after which duty he put on his hat and walked about the place.

Great trees of white lilac rendered the night irresistibly sweet. He paced the narrow paths thinking more of the past than the future. He seemed to stand midway. An almost unbearable sense of loneliness seized him. What would he not have given for his mother's presence at that hour! She who had shared all his aspirations was not there to behold the realization. Such always is life! The planning and striving, and on the achievement, something that bulked huge awanting. Ah! the beauty of that May evening closing in around his new home, and no one to whom to speak to of it. If only Hugh were here! He turned indoors feeling that even a fire would help to bear him company. But Ann had decorated the parlour grate with sprays of "honesty" to signify that fires were out of season. He sought the kitchen. The fire there was carefully raked, and a piece of red turf placed under the ashes where it was expected to "keep in" all night, and in the morning perform the duty of kindling up the fire again.

Bed seemed the only refuge, but the saints failed to answer Ann's prayers regarding sleep. The strangeness of the situation, his new home, his new bed, his new life, overwhelmed and ousted it.

In a field close by a corn-crake delivered its mysterious message to a sleeping world with eloquence. At last it ceased. What a relief! Oliver was actually dozing over when its relative in the next field took up the parable. The effect was slightly fainter but quite as irritating. Then cousins here and there in the distance joined in and passed the night musically in duets, trios, and even for a little time he could detect a quartette. He had just made up his mind that there would not be one wink of sleep for him that night, when he awoke, and lo! it was eight o'clock.

CHAPTER XII

THE FIRST SABBATH IN BALLYDAISY PULPIT

Preach the word; ... reprove, rebuke, exhort.—2nd Tim. iv, 2.

OLIVER felt pleased, when on giving out the 100th Psalm he had allowed his eyes to rest for a moment on the congregation, to see well-filled pews. In truth the "irregulars" had mustered that day. And it was a hot day! Handkerchiefs mopped perspiring foreheads with a certain degree of enjoyment, bonnet strings were untied, and chronic sleepers forced to make an heroic attempt to keep their eyes open.

"Gimme a dunch if you see me goin' over," said Archie Kilpatrick to his wife as the Meeting-house came in sight.

"Shure I'm never done dunchin' you, atween that an' reddin' the weans I don't get much good of the discoorse."

"Well, mebbe you have a clove about you, they're prime for keepin' a body awake in meetin'."

"Here's a peppermint, an' don't cranch it that the whole congregation'll hear you. Many's the time you affront me in meetin' doin' that."

"I wondher will the new man keep us long? That one we had last Sabbath was a tarrible longsome pray-er, I was tired standin'."

"You wouldn't have thought that if you had been rared the way I was—a Covenanter."

"Shure many's the Sabbath Day I just went there to look at you, an' never thought it too long."

"None of your blethers? Here's your halfpenny."

. . . .

The congregation sat during the first psalm. Such was the custom of that time, doubtless originating from the fact that many of them had walked distances and were glad to avail themselves of a rest. To sit at prayer would have seemed an outrage and an insult to Him whom they came to worship. So they stood, turning their backs to the minister. The reading of a chapter from the Old Testament followed, and all except the very youngest followed it in their own Bibles, finding their places with an amount of fissling aided by thumbs dampened on the tongue. This chapter was thoroughly explained as likewise had been the first psalm. A second psalm and a second prayer not so long as the first followed, and then a chapter from the New Testament was read.

These acts were termed the Preliminaries, and merely led up to the climax of the sacred proceedings, which was the sermon. All found the text and fixed their eyes on the pulpit.

It was easily seen that "the new man" was nervous, but that fact did not lessen him in their esteem, especially with the women, for his grey eyes held a beseeching look as though craving for their sympathy. Oliver had not felt so agitated when preaching on trial, but now that he was their chosen he wanted to justify the honour they had done him.

He had written out his sermon and then memorized

it, for the reader of a sermon at Ballydaisy would have been held in contempt, and judged only fit for the Episcopal Church.

Soon, as he warmed to his subject, he forgot his nervousness, so whole-heartedly was he in earnest; holding himself now accountable at the last day for these souls committed to his care, and that it was laid on him to warn them to "flee from the wrath to come". Never did he preach a sermon without pleading with his hearers to accept Christ as their Saviour.

Then followed the announcements: "I intend (God willing) to visit in the townlands of Sturagan and Tullaghacollipy on Tuesday, and will conduct a prayer meeting in Mr. Ephraim Weir's of Tullaghacollipy at seven o'clock."

He then sat down, and an elder on each side of the church rose and armed himself with a collecting-box having a half-lid and a long handle. One wonders why these venerable institutions became extinct. They were eminently suitable for their purpose. Instead of the risky shuffling from hand to hand of a plate or basket, these were safely held by the collector, who without trouble to anyone reaped the pew. Also they were secret as the ballot-box, so that your alms were not "seen of men", if your heart moved you higher than a halfpenny on ordinary Sabbaths, or a thruppeny for special collections. The halfpennies of those days were precious around Ballydaisy, and doubtless precious also in God's sight.

Oliver concluded with a "paraphrase". He had made inquiry and found that there was only one objector—old Timothy Cunningham. While it was being sung Timothy sat ostentatiously reading his Bible, in vainglorious detachment from his surroundings, as who should say: "Let me not be a partner in other men's sins."

No member of Ballydaisy congregation would presume in the public worship of God to sing a "man-made" hymn. But finding the paraphrases bound up in their Bibles, they consequently concluded that these must be at least harmless. Even old Timothy conceded that they were less heinous than hymns. For he had often been heard to declare, that rather than be present within four walls where hymns were sung, he would "worship his Maker under a whin bush".

The stated annual visitation of the congregation just announced did not earn for the minister any special commendation. It was considered obligatory. In order to qualify for the degree of "good visitor", which endeared the ministers of old above all other things to their "people" you were bound in sickness to compete with the doctor. Nay, the doctor was apprised, but the minister by some mysterious sacerdotal telepathy was expected to divine the illness of a member of his flock. He was required to be a prophet, or at least "the son of a prophet".

CHAPTER XIII

THE VISITATION

Wide was his parish, and houses fer asonder.—CHAUCER.

OLIVER had been coached as to the "visitation" in the session-room before the service. This proceeding the new minister was expected to engage in without delay.

"An' of course, I'll go with you," dictated Abram Teggart the elder, "me or Ephraim Weir always went with Mr. Brown, but Ephraim's past that now. I'll acquent you with the people, an' give you an insight intil them; for Mr. Brown knowed them to the very marra' of their bones. He took a dale of saycrets with him when he went, for he sat, an' he sat, an' he listened. For sez he to me once, 'I think it but fair that when I do the talking on Sabbath days and they listen to me with forbearance, that I should allow them the same privilege on other days.' Sir, dear! they tell't him what nayther friend nor neighbour knew, aye, mebbe what husband an' wife didn't tell other. For tell Mr. Brown anything, an' you might as well bury it in the Meetin'-house Green. An' there's a power o' comfort in tellin' what's weighin' on your heart. It makes it on'y half the weight, afther that. An' two tears together, makes truer friendship than all the laughin' an' jokin' in the world.

"Now, there's them I could mention," continued Abram mysteriously, "that talks too much about their own family, an' boastin' of their daughter's music, an' of their grand relations in Belfast, an' like minister like people, for 1st Bannerstown has such a conceit in itself that it's just stinkin' wi' pride. If you just seen them comin' out on a Sabbath day an' meetin' the 2nd Bannerstown people down the street an' lookin' at them as if they were dirt! Not but what Dr. Hill's a good man," Abram hastened to concede, "the root of the matter is in him, but it's past comprehendin' how aisy good Christian men are carried away by bein' mebbe axed to dinner with Epis-copals. A Presbyterian minister should be above the pomps and vanities of this world!"

....

These were the spacious days when clergymen held an annual visitation of every family of the congregation. It occurred as regularly as Christmas or the Twelfth of July. On that day work in the field and household was suspended for the time, the house swept and garnished, and the family and farm servants assembled in the kitchen, if the house could not boast a parlour. This latter was invariably a damp chamber, and usually when the minister arrived was filled with smoke, the chimney being unaccustomed to a fire which was only lighted on ceremonial occasions.

On Tuesday morning Abram Teggart's single tap on the old brass knocker shaped like a gigantic wedding ring, brought Ann from her wash-tub. At first she failed to recognize Abram, never having seen him in Sabbath raiment before.

Oliver was at his morning ritual of garden worship when he felt his tails plucked, and Ann whispered that "Abram Teggart all in black was thonder".

"Did you show him into the parlour?"

"No, I just left him stannin' on the mat."

Oliver brushed past her and found his elder in the exact position that Ann had described. He tried to atone for Ann's incivility, took him into the parlour, and even showed him the bedroom beyond, apologizing meanwhile for the books strewn over both rooms.

"I'm afraid my first stipend must go for bookshelves," he said.

Abram, who with a small farm combined the profession of country carpenter, was eagerly interested.

"Shure I'll do it, an' welcome for ye. Couldn't we stan' them just there atween the fireplace an' the wall an' pent them to look like mahogany? Mr. Brown kep' hees in the other sittin'-room, but you'll be gettin' married, an' the wife'll have to have her drawing-room," he said facetiously. "Mebbe the morra I'll bring down a wheen boords, an' I'll not make much stoor. But we be to start now, Your Reverence, for we have a brave step to go."

The day was hot, but the freshness of early summer was on the trees and hedgerows, and the perfume of newly-cut hay scented the air. Oliver removed his hat and wiped his forehead on which the "kester" had left a red mark. If a minister in those days wore comfortable headgear, his orthodoxy would be wellnigh suspect!

Their road wound along by the shores of Droon Lough, and the large sheet of placid water, with the green "cranoge" in the centre seemed to temper the heat. On the hill above it stood a roofless ivy-clad

Elizabethan castle. Oliver stopped to take in the picturesque scene.

His imagination, always keen, pictured summer mornings of long ago on that lovely spot. He saw chiefs clad in saffron, followed by a crowd of bare-legged retainers, start on such a morning as this for the chase, while fair ladies looked down on them from the loopholes that served for windows in the old stronghold. Next he saw the clash of battle around the walls and the tumult ending in the fire, that only left the enormously thick walls intact.

Other days other manners. It was but a few hundred years since, and here was he an alien of another faith, starting out with his elder for a day's Bible reading and prayer in the same district. Few now of the old clan lived near their earl's castle. The bleak mountainsides and marshy boglands received them while the fertile portions of their inheritance were reserved for the adventurer of another country and another faith.

He was recalled from his daydream by Abram touching him on the arm.

"We must be gettin' on," he said, "the McGillops'll have left their hay, an' they'll be loth to lose this fine day."

....

"They're at the fut of the loanen," announced the herald, in the person of Tommy McGillop, who had been told off to warn the approach of the minister and elder.

Mrs. McGillop as stage-manager frantically made the final preparations.

"Here! yous three sit on the settle," she ordered, giving Tommy and his two sisters a shove in that direction with a powerful hand. Then she dragged her coarse apron from its protecting office over her Sabbath dress, and smoothed the already flat hair on each side of her forehead.

"Why, where on earth's your da?" she demanded excitedly. "He should be on the street to meet the ministher. What soort of manners will he think we have! Look out if you see any signs of him in the hag-yard, Tommy."

Tommy peeped out of the tiny window behind the settle and announced that his da was busy there.

Mrs. McGillop sprang to the window, and with strong knuckles on the glass compelled instant attention. With desperate pantomimic gestures, accompanied by a scowling countenance, she succeeded in conveying to her husband in forcible sign language of her own the command to convey himself instantly to the other side of the house, and receive the minister ceremoniously.

The children on the settle were impressed with the momentousness of the occasion. Little seven-year-old Maggie had a dire feeling of awe that pulled down the corners of her rosy mouth, and enlarged her blue eyes. Tommy did not fail to seize the opportunity of trading on her apprehensions.

"Just wait, me girl, till he asks you your catechism, an' if you don't know it oul' Mr. Teggart'll take you away. That's what he brings him for. He carries the sack."

Maria, while joining in the fun against Maggie, felt her own courage diminish as she mumbled over and over to herself the jumble of sounds constituting answers to questions in the "Shorter Catechism", which conveyed no more meaning to her mind than one of Horace's odes in the original, but which by Presbyterian practice and tradition she was compelled to learn by heart. Truth to tell Tommy's banter was for the most part the proverbial whistling in a graveyard, his nervousness taking the boyish form of bullying someone else.

The three victims on the settle sat on. Through the open door they heard their father who by dint of a sprint from the hag-yard had reached in time the correct spot where a minister should be received. Mrs. McGillop herself stood at the door and advanced a few steps. "I bid you welcome to Sturaghan," she said, extending her hand and shaking Oliver's up and down several times. Her husband had merely remarked that it was a "tarrable warm day", and then considered his duty done. Once "Margit" was on the scene Daniel's social responsibilities ended.

The atmosphere was tense on the settle as the mother named her three offsprings to the minister, and bade them rise up and shake hands. Mr. Teggart also shook hands with them, a ceremony that never took place from one visitation to another. In fact, early that morning Tommy had met Mr. Teggart on the bog road. Mr. Teggart remarked, "Is that you?" Tommy said "Aye." And that was all there was about it.

Mrs. McGillop dusted a chair for the minister, and in a more perfunctory way one for the elder, and there fell a calm on that wide pleasant kitchen usually the scene of incessant bustle, and a sense of peaceful rest as the spiritual for the time banished the material.

After some very tender conversation about their beloved old friend and minister, Mrs. McGillop handed a Bible to the new minister, and the solemn exercises began.

"Behold what manner of love the Father hath bestowed upon us that we should be called the sons of God. … Beloved now are we the sons of God, and it doth not appear what we shall be, but we know when He shall appear, we shall be like Him for we shall see Him as he is. …

"See God! Can mortal grasp that predication? These his lowly servants toiling in fields and kitchens and now kneeling on the earthen floor in adoration, if kept by His Grace, would one day see Him as He is! That promise makes of the lowliest life committed to His keeping a triumphal progress on a King's highway, not to a grave but to a celestial palace!

"May these dear children," Oliver prayed, "give their young hearts into Thy keeping, and grow up noble and pure and good, so that their lives in after years may witness for Thee their Lord and Saviour. May we all be called the 'Sons of God', so that when this swiftly passing life is ended we shall indeed 'see Him as He is'."

There ensued that mystic silence that a prayer leaves behind it for some time after they rose from their knees, until the minister began to ask the children friendly questions about school, and they actually were getting quite at ease in this awesome person's presence, when their mother, who never seemed to forget anything, produced a catechism. He asked them a few questions, prompting them in the answers when necessary, and taking little Maggie on his knee, he told her of a child Who was once King of Glory, and Who loved little children and loves them still.

Afterwards the talk ran on crops and poor prices. Oliver told them he had been brought up on a farm, and knew well all they had to contend with. Daniel got quite conversational, and invited him out to "have a look at the kettle", and on leaving, the whole household "convoyed" him to the "fut of the loanen", and returned uplifted in heart and mind to the common round of their life, more quickened to the sense of God's Presence with them and all their concerns. Nothing wins hearts for the Kingdom like the personal touch, which was the method of our Great Exemplar.

As they mounted the hill that led to the home of his next hearer Abram beguiled the climb by a character sketch.

"This one is a middle-aged girl called Ellen Orr. She knows her Bible off by heart, an' she could talk the legs off a pot. She's a doncy crayther, always complainin', but she's never as bad as she thinks herself. But she's a dacent good girl, an' well respected by everybody for her kerechter."

The diminutive cottage by the roadside shone dazzlingly white, for "the twelfth" was near, and the loyal honoured its approach by copious use of whitewash and glaring paint. One could easily recognize a "Protestant" neighbourhood by these signs.

Ellen stood by the door watching for her visitors, and Abram made the introduction politely. "This is Miss Orr—Mr. Whiteside." Oliver felt his hand grasped, warmly shaken, and led inside. The two men seemed to fill the tiny kitchen which was spotless—the dresser, table, and wag-at-the-wall clock, all painted bright red. There were only two chairs—also painted red—which were "set forrad" for the minister and elder, Ellen seating herself on a "creepie" beside them.

To Oliver's consternation she immediately threw her apron over her head, and began to cry loudly. He would have felt alarmed, had not Abram smiled reassuringly at him, to indicate that Ellen was "emotional". In a few minutes the apron was removed, and Ellen explained.

"Yous two comin', put me in mind of Mr. Brown, an' I couldn't keep in. I just filled up. A shakehands from Mr. Brown was worth another body's sarmon. Them that knew Mr. Brown'll never forget him till the breath laves their body! When he went I thought I would never get over it. Och Oh! Och Oh!"

"Mr. Teggart tells me," said the minister, "that your health is not all that could be desired."

"I may say I never knowed what good health was," said Ellen proudly. "Why the very minute I set eyes on ye I took a touch o' wakeness. I don't rightly know what ails me at the present time. I have nayther pain nor ache, but I just stopped atin'."

"You'll be mended an' walkin' on the 'twelfth'," said Abram.

"Is it me! I couldn't thravel the len'th of the field if they were to make me an Orangeman. But Dear sen' they'll get a fine day, for what would we do on'y for them, shure we'd be murthered in our beds, so we would. But mebbe I'll hear the drums an' that quare an' heartsome. Not but what I have the best of Catholic neighbours, for there never was a neighbour yet that I couldn't spake to, no, I never fell out wi' nobody, not one of them but would carry me on their backs if I needed it."

Oliver tried to stem the current by inquiring if she had any relatives, or if she lived alone.

"Aye, just me lief lone. But there's worse ways o' livin' nor that. Once I was tarrible near gettin' married an' him a convarted man like myself, but he took a decline an' died, for, like the ass in Scripture, 'the Lord had need of him.' "

At this information Oliver sought his handkerchief and blew his nose while Ellen continued:

"Summer was a year a niece from Ameriky come an' stayed wi' me, an' indeed an' doubles I'm tellin' you no lie, I was glad to see the back seam of her stockin'. She had a thrunk that set there atween the jamb-wall an' the windy, an' it would bate you to get in or out past it. An' what was it? Just a box o' vanity! Now, sez I till her, 'them outfits may do for Ameriky, but mind now that you're in a God fearin' land an' don't darr to enther Ballydaisy Meetin'-house in one of them "keowboys".' They were just what the Bible calls 'vain apparel'."

"Get Mr. Whiteside a Bible, Ellen," said Abram, "till he reads a chapter."

"Here it is on the shelf over me head, five an' thirty times I've read it from Genesis to Revelation. I'm at Habbakuk at the present, but I'll never finish it this time, for I'm just one day bad an' the next day worse, an' the docther sez he can do nothin' more for me, for 'Ellen', sez he, 'you have got a share of every bottle I ever had in the dispensary.' This one here on the dresser is the one I'm at now. Would you taste a sup of it? This docther keeps the best of bottles—not like the one was here afore him. They said he just filled a crock wi' spring wather an' put some laudanum, an' plenty of peppermint, an' filled all the bottles out of that agin dispensary day. You would think it was a dhrink o' pleasure you were takin'. Now what good is a bottle, unless it bees so bitther that you be to girn to get it down. *That* surprises your inside an taches it a lesson."

"The 1st chapter of 2nd Corinthians," announced the minister, and read it to the end. After the prayer that followed, Oliver stood, meaning to signify that they were departing, but Ellen had much more to communicate.

"Afther all," she resumed, "my niece was a brave wee girl, an' left me a good bit o' money when she went, an' I have a goat, for there's nothin' improves tay like a sup of goat's milk in it. An' I keep hens, not that I could lip an egg meself, for sez the docther to me, 'Ellen, your liver wouldn't stan' an egg, but dhrink lashins o' butthermilk.' I kep' a cow once, but I had to part with her for she ate everything she could lay her han's on. The last thing she done on me was to chaw up the corner of Mrs. McTrusty's best tablecloth, that was bleachin' on the hedge, the one she puts down when the ministher goes for his dinner, the way you're doin' the day. So that finished Molly, an' I got Paddy McGladrigan to sell her for me in th' Moy fair, an' I have the price of her past me to bury me dacent—a hearse wi' white rockets, an' a white linen scarf with a black rosette for the ministher an' one for the docther."

Oliver kept moving to the door suggestively.

"Isn't it well yous come a day I was middlin' at all, an' that yous didn't get me crulged over the fire an' not able to spake to ye?"

Oliver's hand was now on the latch. "Well, good-bye," he said, "and I hope you'll keep well till I see you again."

"Good-bye, Mr. Whiteside. You done me a dale o' good talkin' till me. I feel betther already. God's blessing on you an' may you be as the Scripture says 'a nail in the right place'. It's not every Sabbath Day I can thravel to Ballydaisy Meetin', for I'm just one day bad, an' the next day worse. ..."

They extricated themselves in the middle of a sentence.

A few fields only separated them from James McTrusty's. Mrs. McTrusty always claimed the honour of entertaining the minister to dinner on a day of visitation in Sturaghan townland.

It was a "full" place. You could scarcely catch a glimpse of the snug thatched cottage by reason of the fat haystacks in the hag-yard, and the pyramid of turf that reared its head in defiance of the Northern winter.

The arrivals were heralded by a fanfare of barking and quacking and cackling and grunting that caused Mrs. McTrusty to rush out. "Chew, Chew," she entreated the large black dog, while with a swish of her apron sideways and a "sssh", she scattered an army of hens and ducks to right and left. How welcome the minister was in every home! Oliver was touched by the sincerity and openheartedness of it all.

Their hostess led them across the kitchen and into "the room". A large round table occupied the centre whereupon on ordinary days was enthroned the family Bible, while around it at intervals were symmetrically arranged a few books of the baser sort.

To-day the literature had given place to a snow-white cloth on which were laid black-handled knives and forks. Mrs. McTrusty was a notable housekeeper, and there had never been any little feet to carry "clabber" in, as she called it, on her clean floors, nor any tiny restless hands to pull things awry. Year by year she had cherished tidiness and cleanliness until they were now her household gods. Indeed she judged others of her sex according as they kept "a clean house", or the reverse. An ironic writer has left posterity the oft-quoted aphorism that "cleanliness is next to godliness". A multitude of womankind go farther and put it before it.

"James is in the far lan'," she said, "but he'll be home any minute now. Isn't it the quare warm day. Me clothes is just stickin' to me back."

There was a deafening clatter of horses and carts. Her husband and the "servant-boy" swept on to the "street", at which Mrs. McTrusty excused herself, and hastened from the room to intercept James from walking straight for "the presence" with the odours of the field upon him.

"Here!" she commanded, pouring a kettleful of

scalding water into a tin basin, and handing him a pound of yellow soap. "Clean yourself well, an' slip on this coat and weskit." She knew it was useless to request him to change his nether corduroy garments.

"What about your boots? You didn't half knock the clabber off them afore you come in. Here, pull on your good ones for the time bein' and when James, under some feeble protest, had fulfilled these injunctions, she said, "Now go in an' talk to the ministher while I dish up the dinner."

James was a tall thin man with high cheek bones and bright blue eyes, a straggling bit of sandy hair grew under his chin. He was intelligent and read everything that came his way. His wife disapproved entirely of reading on weekdays. She said she "never knowed them that read books to keep a clean house". Most people have an eleventh commandment. Hers was, "Thou must keep a clean house."

James could talk on politics and ecclesiastical matters, as well as of soils and crops and manures. He and the minister were having a good "crack", when the door was thrust open by Mrs. McTrusty's foot, her hands being taken up with a large dish, on which lay side by side a roast fowl and a chunk of roast beef. Her next journey produced a mountain of potatoes and a lavish dish of green peas.

When the four were seated, the hostess wiped the perspiration from her face, and requested the minister to "ask a blessing", after which she carved and her husband conversed.

"I'm tol'," he said, "there's eight on the list for Second Bannerstown; they're at the seventh now, an' they hardly mind what the first one was like."

"It's but a middlin' sort of place an' dwindlin' at that," said Abram Teggart, "an' of coorse the Reverend McConkey'll keep the Manse."

"He will *that* an' no mistake," said James, "afther marryin' three weemen with money, an' for all that it just goes to his heart to part with a thruppeny bit."

"Well, he's near done now, an' he can't take it with him," remarked Abram sententiously.

"No, for it might be melted," said James.

Mrs. McTrusty frowned at her husband. James's jokes might shock the new minister!

"Poor Mr. McConkey has got a bit deef," she said, as if this affliction excused avariciousness.

"Aye, an' if you asked him for money he can hear none at all," put in James.

"He has had a dale of trouble in his life," said Mrs. McTrusty, "his daughter married a Churchman, an' this is his third wife, the other two are buried in Second Bannerstown Green, an' I suppose this one'll lie there too; it's his custom to bury his wives there."

"Well," commented her husband, "there'll be what they call a 'stour' at the resurrection!

Mrs. McTrusty did not smile, but she changed the subject adroitly. "How's your mistress, Abram?"

"Bravely, but she bees very notionate about her meat. I tell her she'll soon be an oul' crock like Ellen Orr."

"How's Ellen the day?"

"Oh! her tongue's as souple as ever. I think it'll not give up till the daisies is growin' out of her eyes."

"She was always a rale good girl," defended Mrs. McTrusty, "an' kep' everything roun' her protestant lookin', both inside an' outside."

"Oh, aye!" agreed Abram, "she could keep everythin' shinin' with a spittle."

While this discussion was going on, Oliver was courageously attacking the pile of chicken and beef allotted him, yet when he laid down his knife and fork there was consternation.

"I doubt your dinner wasn't to your likin'," lamented his hostess.

"It was excellent," said Oliver.

James went to a diamond-paned cupboard in the corner and brought out a bottle and glasses.

"None for me, thank you," said the minister.

"But it's good port wine," said James surprised.

"I don't take any sort, I'm a teetotaller."

"Well, to be shure! I heerd tell of them, but you're the first ever I seen."

"I hope I'll not be the last, for I intend to enlist all I can."

"You'll never be a betther man than Mr. Brown, an' he always took a glass after his dinner."

"He was one in a thousand that could do that and not exceed. We must abstain for the sake of the weaker brethren as well as our own. We never know how it may end even with ourselves."

"I'm with you there, Mr. Whiteside," said Mrs. McTrusty. "I never seen any good it done, but a dale of harm. Many's a time James comes home from the market, an' on'y the'oul mare knows the road, the Dear knows what shough he would be found in."

"Now, there's the Reverend Hagan," said James, "an' on sacrament Sundays, him an' the elders drink what's left over."

"That's an old custom I thought had died out in

these enlightened times. Poor Mr. Hagan belongs to a former generation, but we must begin and educate the young."

"You'll not refuse a dhrop, Abram?" said James.

"I'm an old man, too, an' can't change my way of goin', let them that's young do what they have a mind, but I'm afeared Mr. Whiteside'll not get many to side wi' him."

"I am convinced I am in the right," said Oliver, "and what are we ministers for but to improve the world and hasten Christ's kingdom."

The servant-boy was now called in for "worship", and this concluded, the minister and elder left, after a very cordial farewell.

"That one would fight," said James to his wife when their visitors were out of hearing. "I b'lieve we didn't go far wrong in takin' him."

"Aye, he's not one of the mealy-mouthed sort that's just whatever anybody is that's talkin' to them," said Mrs. McTrusty approvingly. "The Ballydaisy people should thank the Lord for sendin' them a *man*!"

....

The minister and his elder had two more visits to pay before arriving at Ephraim Weir's, where the prayer-meeting was to be held. Here the kitchen was seated with chairs borrowed from neighbouring houses. Old people near who were not able to "travel" to Ballydaisy on Sabbaths availed themselves of the privilege of hearing the Gospel once more. Others who "never darkened a church door", often attended these informal services. Oliver got to love these prayer-meetings, and his heart went out to the toilers who, after a hard day's work, had "cleaned themselves" and come to listen to the Word. Never was he more conscious of the Master's Presence than at these simple gatherings of the "two or three" in humble farmhouse kitchens.

CHAPTER XIV

VISITORS

The only way to have a friend is to be one. — EMERSON.

"NOW, Mamma," said Eleanor Hill at the breakfast table a few weeks after the ordination in Ballydaisy, "we must give a party and introduce the newcomer to the neighbourhood."

"It means a lot of trouble," sighed Mrs. Hill, "but, of course, it is our duty, your father being minister of the most important congregation in the Presbytery. What do you say, Papa?"

Dr. Hill, however, was deep in the contents of a letter that had arrived by the post, and was unaware of the subject under discussion. When the project was explained to him he gravely considered it "the right and proper thing to do".

"Strange to say," he went on, "this letter is written to me on behalf of this young man of whom we are now speaking. It is from Dr. Morgan, requesting me to show him any kindness in my power, and speaking in very high terms as to his character and diligence. Here is what he says:" — Dr. Hill cleared his throat, and read aloud — " 'I have formed a very high opinion of Mr. Whiteside's mental and moral worth, and am fully persuaded that he takes up the work of the Ministry from the one motive that alone justifies it as a profession.' He sends you his kind regards, my dear," he added to his wife.

Mrs. Hill looked very much gratified. This kind

message seemed to brace her for her duty to the new ministerial brother.

"I wonder if he'll know how to behave at it," said Eleanor's brother.

"Well, Edward," said his father reprovingly, "that may not be *his* fault. He probably has not had your advantage in the social scale. He is, I am told, a farmer's son, but so also are the majority of our ministers." Dr. Hill spoke as one of exalted distinction. He himself was the son of a minister who was the son of a farmer.

"We have to ask the Watsons anyway," said Mrs. Hill, who conceived that her life calling was to entertain. "Indeed, they should have been asked long ago, but she has never returned my visit."

"Likely doesn't know she should," suggested Edward.

"Well," said his mother, "I was told she had a fortune of a thousand pounds, and you would think anyone with such a fortune would know that much."

"Your plan," said the doctor, "would be to write to Mrs. Watson and say that you will waive ceremony in the matter, and invite her for a certain evening. That will give her (if she be ignorant in the matter) a hint of what is necessary in the case." Dr. Hill was a leader in the General Assembly by reason of diplomatic council tendered to that body in his heavily important manner.

"I hope she'll know to put on her wedding dress, for, of course, we'll have to ask the Wallingtons and the Scandretts. When you have Episcopalians it makes you a little uncomfortable to have Presbyterians too. How would it do to have two evenings? One for the quality, and one for the Presbyterian ministers and their wives. The same cooking would do. Have the Episcopalians one evening, and what they leave would do the Presbyterians the next."

"Eleanor!" Her father's tone conveyed rebuke enough, while Mrs. Hill put on a pained expression, and Edward smiled to himself in the shocked silence that ensued. It was difficult to imagine how good Dr. and Mrs. Hill came to have such a mischievous daughter!

In a few moments the dignified doctor regained his equilibrium. "Let us settle on an evening at once," he said, "and as I am going in that direction this morning, I shall pay my call on Mr. Whiteside, and at the same time give him your invitation."

They went into committee. Monday—washing day—was, of course, out of the question. Tuesday would be required for preparations. Wednesday was the prayer-meeting. The choice lay between Thursday and Friday, but the latter approached rather closely the Sabbath, and Dr. Hill was not the man to leave his preparation to the last minute. Thursday was evidently the predestined day, and Thursday it was decided.

....

As the Rev. Oliver Whiteside was about to sit down to his modest one o'clock dinner, a knock at the Manse door reverberated through the house. Such a distinguished "double knock" as he had not been honoured with hitherto, and immediately after, Ann's head was thrust in at the door.

"It's a tarrable gran' clargyman in a kesther hat," she said softly. "What on earth'll we do!"

Oliver, too, was at a loss how to act in the emergency. For all he knew it might be the rector of the parish, and Ann, he noticed, economized in the washing of tablecloths. Also his meagre dish of boiled bacon and cabbage would not admit of offering either as regarded quality or quantity.

"Whip it intil your bedroom," suggested the inspired Ann, "while I'm lettin' him in, an' I'll keep him dallyin' at the door." Ann's type of cleverness shone in a situation like the present.

His hands grasping the slippery crockery, Oliver listened, and heard an imposing voice that instantly recalled "the charge", inquiring if Mr. Whiteside were in.

Before Ann's guarded reply reached him, the joint of bacon slid from its dish that he had held aslant, and fell at his feet. Oliver was conscious by this time that the visitor had stepped into the hall, and that Ann by way of "dallyin' " was urging him to divest himself of his "topcoat". Giving the frolicsome bacon a vigorous kick that sent it to hide under the cover of the easy-chair, he quickly thrust the other dishes on the floor of his bedroom, and shut the door. The visitor did not seem to be responding to Ann's suggestion regarding the "topcoat", in fact he had none on, and Ann knew this, but anything to prolong the conversation in the hall.

The tablecloth remained! Fearing that he dared not open his bedroom door again, lest the other door opposite should open simultaneously, with an inspiration that surprised himself when he thought of it afterwards he stuffed the cloth up the chimney.

He heard Ann saying, "That's the quare purty dog

you have, Your Reverence, would it be a coley?" and at that a large black mongrel dashed into the room followed by his master, Dr. Hill.

The doctor apologized profusely for the timing of his visit, he had business in the neighbourhood, and wished to be back for dinner at three o'clock, and also for the dog's intrusion—he had followed him unawares, and had not shown himself until they were a long way from home—he hoped Mr. Whiteside would forgive him for calling during morning hours.

Oliver begged him to be seated in the only armchair he possessed, and himself sat opposite by the window.

Dr. Hill wiped his forehead with a very white and very large handkerchief, remarking that the day was rather "oppressive".

Oliver said, he feared it would probably be thunder before evening.

The doctor trusted Mr. Whiteside was satisfied with his new sphere of work, and hoped he had already made the acquaintance of many of his congregation. "I believe you will find them a peaceable community," said the doctor patronizingly, "and there is no doubt they were very much attached to their late lamented minister—a most worthy man, Mr. Whiteside—lie down, Fido, lie down— —" this last remark was addressed to the black mongrel that was working itself up to a high degree of excitement, and sniffing around the doctor's chair.

"We ministers," he went on, "have an enormous responsibility—you don't happen to keep a cat, do you? Cats always excite Fido, and I thought there might perhaps be one concealed beneath the chair."

Oliver assured him there was not a cat in his establishment.

"It behoves us ministers," resumed Dr. Hill, "to be both active and prayerful"; and it occurred to Oliver, that he had been unwontedly active a few minutes ago, while his sincerest prayer at that moment was that his visitor's dog might be diverted from its inquisitiveness.

The doctor delivered Mrs. Hill's message in genial yet imposing manner.

"We intend having a few friends for the evening on Thursday next—the seventeenth. We ministers enjoy the social amenities as do others. Intercourse with the refined and educated is most helpful. We shall also have a little music—my daughter is quite gifted in that way—by the way, she informs me she has had the pleasure of meeting you when at school in Belfast—also our young brother, Mr. Summers, of Klergymore, has a decided talent for elocution, and will I hope contribute to the evening's innocent relaxation. We hope, too, to have with us a school friend of my daughter's, a Miss Hester Temple, whom she expects this very morning. I fancy I heard my daughter say this young lady was a friend of yours."

Oliver thanked the doctor and Mrs. Hill for their kind invitation, and accepted it with an inward fervour of which the good doctor was unconscious. He on his part offered some hospitality—a cup of tea—Ann would have it in in a few minutes, he promised recklessly.

The doctor thanked him politely, but declined.

"I make it a rule not to eat between stated meals. We dine at three o'clock, so must hasten. Why, Fido, what are you eating?"

Oliver artfully drew the doctor's attention from Fido's conduct, by asking him if he did not think there was a fine view from the window, and rose as if to show it off. His visitor also advanced to survey it the better.

Before them stretched the "blue hills of Tyrowen", and the well-wooded landscape sloping to a silver streak on the horizon that was Lough Neagh.

Dr. Hill regarded the scene solemnly for some moments, and then gave his judgment.

"The view from your house, Mr. Whiteside, is elevating, elevating indeed."

Whilst his visitor was immersed in the beauties of nature, Oliver stole a hasty glance behind his back just in time to witness the final disappearance of his and Ann's dinner. It was somewhat of a loss, yet its departure relieved him and made him feel more cordial to his august visitor, and he begged him to be seated once more, so that Dr. Hill came away quite predisposed in his "young brother's" favour.

Oliver would have considered it discourteous not to have accompanied a guest to the gate. But when he got the doctor and Fido dispatched safely through it, and turned back, he gave way to the uncontrollable laughter that he had so long repressed. Ann's seriously inquiring face at the doorstep only added fuel to his mirth.

"I have the things brought back out of the bedroom, but I can't find the bacon nowhere," she announced, and when her master could not explain for laughter, she got quite annoyed. At last he managed to say:

"It's gone. It fell off the dish, and the dog ate it."

"An' did you not sthrive to pull it from him?"

"No," confessed Oliver, helpless with laughter.

"An' did thon clargyman stan' by an' see our dinner ate up on us?"

Oliver tried to explain that Dr. Hill didn't see it, but Ann apparently could not believe him. The magnitude of her loss weighed heavily on her, as she retreated with angry mutterings of "him an' his oul' pickpocket of a dog."

Suddenly she turned sharply. "Did he ate the tablecloth, too?" she demanded.

"I'll get it for you," promised Oliver, guiltily unwilling in face of Ann's intense indignation to disclose its lurking-place, "you see in the hurry I just had to stuff it up the chimney."

Ann quickened her step as if rescue at the earliest moment was imperative. She dragged it forth whilst Oliver now getting into a more sober frame of mind watched fearfully to see the consequences of his rash act.

Ann's comments on it, however, might have led one to believe that its purity had been immaculate previous to the fatal moment of its introduction to the chimney. Eventually she gave her opinion that it wasn't so "overly" bad, and would do till the end of the week. She also magnanimously gave her master to know that her displeasure didn't rest on him, that he was merely the victim of the net spread for him by Dr. Hill and his "blagyard of a dog". So she spread the besmirched linen again on the table, and said generously that she would fry him a bit of bacon and an egg. Oliver thanked her as generously, and sat down in the doctor's chair with a book to await it.

Scarcely had he started the deferred meal, his book propped up before him as his habit was, that he was conscious of something of the nature of a scuffle in the hall. Someone had evidently taken the liberty of walking in by the open door, and Ann seemed to be intercepting their entrance. Thus he interpreted the situation by the sounds.

"Just step in here a minute," he heard her saying, opening the door on the other side of the hall, and of course revealing emptiness beyond.

"But isn't he in the other room?"

Ann admitted that was so. "But mebbe he's at his devotions," she cautioned.

"Not a fear of that."

Oliver's heart bounded at the voice, and in a second he was in the hall.

"Hugh, man, but I'm glad to see you."

"It looks uncommonly like it," said Hugh smiling.

"Why didn't you tell me you were coming, and I would have had something for your dinner?"

"Hester was coming to the Hills, and at the last moment I thought it my duty to come with her. I had not the face to go in, but left her at the gate and rushed on to you."

"Well, you must have something to eat, for you had an early start. Ann, would you please fry some more bacon and an egg."

Ann, who meanwhile had stood by an avowed listener to the conversation, now went close to her master's ear and whispered something.

"All right!" said Hugh, "I'll just take the half of His Reverence's."

Another plate of bacon was forthcoming, and the egg halved.

"I'm afraid the potatoes are cold," said the host.

"They are," said the guest cheerfully.

"The tablecloth met with an accident," further apologized the host.

"It was a serious one," said the guest.

Their laughter rang through the house, as Oliver related the drama of Dr. Hill's visit, and burst at intervals into the kitchen.

"He's a brother for sure," Ann said to herself, "didn't I see he favoured His Riverence the minute I clapped eyes on him."

. . . .

Later, they sat in the summer-house talking over old days at college. McKittuck, who was always talking about culture, had at last got a wee place called Tullyspade. "He'll find plenty of culture there, but it will be agriculture," remarked Hugh. "Jenkinson (Demosthenes, they called him) had never got a place yet. Dilly was married last week to five thousand, but God help him!" said Hugh, "she has the looks of a stickin' cow. And George– –" their voices betrayed them–"George would never preach again!" The world was to be left to the Jenkinsons and the Dillys, and George, the man they loved and needed, nay, that the world called aloud for, had even now left it for ever."

"Come and take a look at my wee cow."

They passed through a little gate that led from the garden to the Manse fields.

"Your potatoes look grand," said Hugh.

"They're doing well. The congregation planted them in faith not knowing who would eat thereof. I expect to be digging them about the twelfth."

A little harmless cow stared over the hedge at them in a friendly way.

"She's a moiley," said Hugh.

"She is, and a fine wee mountainy cow. I got her in Bannerstown fair for four pounds ten. Wait till you taste her cream! I also possess six hens and three ducks. Come into the yard and I'll show them to you."

"I doubt," said Hugh, "Hezekiah's example is no warning to you. You seem to glory in showing off your treasures to visitors from a far country."

"Yes, and I'm going to show my visitor off too. I have announced a Temperance Meeting in Innis schoolhouse to-night, and intend you to support me."

"I suppose you're taking up 'Total Abstinence'."

"Certainly. To-night I am going to proclaim myself a teetotaller. I cannot do otherwise," said Oliver simply.

"If it had been eight hundred years ago you would have been away on Moiley's back for the Holy Land."

"Crusaders will be needed to the millennium," said Oliver. "But, Hugh, you'll stand by me to-night, won't you? I believe everyone thinks I am a confident young person, but they little know how shaky I am through it all, and how depressed I get at times."

"Oh! I'll go with you, but you needn't expect me

to speak on the subject, for I haven't got the length of refusing a glass of wine yet."

"Well," said Oliver, "I have taken my last."

CHAPTER XV

THE TEMPERANCE MEETING

And when the last Great Scorer comes
  To write against your name,
He'll ask not if you won or lost,
  But how you played the game.

THERE were many curious glances at the two young ministers as they walked down to the schoolhouse in Innis. This was indeed something new—this Temperance Movement—and beyond the bounds of possibility. But the minister was young, he meant well, and there would be no harm in going, anyway, thought some. Others, however, members of Ballydaisy congregation were actually in the trade, and were the real lions in Oliver's path; but he told himself that those who enlisted for Christ's Kingdom must never shirk a fight.

Sabbath after Sabbath immediately the minister gave out his text, no matter in what part of the Bible it lay, the boy Oliver would turn up 1st Samuel, 17th chapter. Indeed he scarcely needed to go to that trouble, for his Bible opened of its own accord at that page. Recorded there was surely the most glorious exploit in history—the killing of the Giant by the boy David. Oliver, secure behind his mother's shoulder, gloated on the words of his young hero, "when all the men of Israel fled and were sore afraid"—"Thy servant will go and fight with this Philistine!" A resounding thump on the pulpit cushion would cause him to look upwards.

Mr. Birch was perchance vigorously repudiating the "Antinomian" heresy and quoting profusely from "The Marrow of Divinity" to defend his case. How tame it all was compared with the fascinating field of action lying on his knee. Thrilled for the hundredth time Oliver would read, "David ran and stood upon the Philistine" — stood upon him! wasn't that superb! "And took his sword out of the sheath thereof, and cut off his head therewith." Oliver almost smacked his lips. That was the apex of daring achievement, to cut off the head of the inflated scoundrel with his very own sword.

In after life when the man Oliver essayed to fight giants he used to say that the 17th chapter of 1st Samuel was the chapter in the Bible he knew best.

....

A fair attendance was gathered, largely of young people to whom chance meetings of any sort meant a rendezvous. He had asked Wm. Moynagh as a personal favour to be present as the leading man of the place.

"But I can take a drop myself," William had smilingly replied.

"I might possibly persuade you to give it up."

"Not me! I have to take my glass with a good customer. My business would soon go to the dogs if I took up these notions. No, I couldn't go myself, but I tell you what I'll do, I'll send Adam and Willie, an' mebbe Annie might go; she would if she thought it was anything good; for if ever I ever get to heaven, it'll be on her account. Make Willie a teetotaller if you like, his father made a bad hand of it."

The schoolhouse felt like an oven. The window

panes were misted with a coat of heat, and the candles in their sconces around the walls, which might be necessary later, had changed their normal position and gazed dejectedly at the floor.

Oliver always liked a meeting to commence with singing, but he knew he would have to raise the tune himself and his repertoire consisted of only one—"Martyrdom." Other tunes he might and did join in, but could not produce unaided. He had already confided this difficulty to Hugh on the way and said: "Don't you sing too strong beside me Hugh, for it doesn't take much to put me off the tune."

"I don't think you're much better than myself at it," retorted Hugh, "and I'd advise you not to try it at all."

"Oh, I'm sound on 'Martyrdom', and it's a great mercy, for it fits most of the psalms, the long measures are beyond me. I wish I could do the old hundredth, but I never could manage it alone."

On the backless forms facing the speaker sat the females, while the male portion of the audience ranged themselves along the side wall.

As Oliver, perspiring, was thankfully bringing the twenty-third Psalm and "Martyrdom" to a fairly successful conclusion aided by a few weak feminine voices, Adam Clements who did his best to sustain the minister on one low note, received a "dunch" from Willie Moynagh that caused him to raise his eyes from his psalm-book. A vision of perfect loveliness to poor Adam's eyes in the person of Miss Martha McIlroy followed her aunt Mrs. Tuffit up the schoolhouse to where there were vacant seats at the front. Yellow hair like honey and red cheeks like roses, what more thought Adam could mortal man desire! Thus dazzled, he turned round after the last word of the psalm and stared at the wall, in what he considered the proper posture for prayer.

He was conscious of Willie pulling his coat tails, first gently, and then with increasing violence. For a time he paid no attention, used to Willie's mischievous performances, but as the tugging persisted he got angry, and stooping to Willie who was seated said, "Wait till I go home an' I'll larn your uncle of your behavor."

Willie, he noticed, tried to speak, but seemed unable, he being shaken with suppressed mirth, yet withal he kept on pulling at Adam's coat tails.

Adam stooped again. "You're actin' like a haythen," he whispered, "isn't it time you larned to listen to a prayer?"

So ashamed was Adam of Willie's conduct, that he glanced round to see if anyone was noticing it. There in the very front seat sat his lovely Martha, her head indeed bowed, but with laughter also. Even Mrs. Tuffit appeared to be smiling and was holding her handkerchief up to her mouth. The whole audience in fact seemed to be in an inexplicable state of mirth, considering the fact that they were supposed to be praying.

Adam wondered what Mr. Whiteside thought of such scandalous conduct, and glancing round in his direction, wondered to see even his own minister with his hand over his mouth as if to conceal it.

Lastly, his eyes fell on the strange young minister who was standing behind the desk reading from an open Bible, the only person in the room apparently who saw nothing funny. Then Adam grasped the awful situation. He had turned his back, and was fervently praying while all the time the minister was merely reading a chapter! Oh! Martha, what have you not to answer for?

Quicker than anything he had ever done in his life before, Adam sat down, and wished he could go through the floor, or that the roof might fall and hide him from view at that terrible moment. But no miracle occurred to oblige him, and after a long time he attempted to raise his degraded head, and perceived that the elders had resumed control of their faces; yet the eyes in the fair face that had been the cause of his humiliation were still dancing.

This small unrehearsed farce put the audience in good humour for the novel lecture.

It is difficult now to estimate the courage of the pioneer teetotaller clergy. They were "a voice crying in the wilderness", their ideals scarcely comprehended. Nevertheless they clung to them in spite of bufferings. Most disagreeable task of all was the rebuking of members of their congregations who were in the trade. For at that time small public houses dotted the country districts, many of them owned by strict Presbyterians.

Oliver was endowed with the soul of the reformer—he whose whole being shrieks at evils which others calmly accept. Many ministers did indeed preach "Moderation in all things", lopping gracefully at the branches. He felt he must off with his coat and hack at the root, of necessity obeying an inner voice that told him "This is your day's work".

It is a proof of the divine in man that human

hearts respond intuitively to the genuine, while all the sanctimoniousness paraded in lieu of this is taken at its exact value. It is infinitely easier to deceive oneself than it is to impose on others. Oliver had no really brilliant gifts, but he was incapable of dissimulation. Honesty towards God and man was in his heart. This was recognized, and he won where others failed.

He now earnestly put the subject of Temperance before his listeners, showed the gigantic evils caused by intoxicating drink to body and soul, and warned the young from falling or drifting as they usually do into its deadly clutches.

When he had finished his address, and sat down he felt as on all like occasions depressed and conscious of shortcoming. If he had only been granted the gift of oratory! He did not realize that the earnestness which always carried him away when on his feet had more lasting effect than a mere flashy "delivery".

What, therefore, was his surprise to hear Hugh who had risen say:

"I came here to-night just because my friend Mr. Whiteside asked me to do so. I had not thought much on the matter, but as he has so convincingly reasoned the question, and so fervently pleaded with us all to sign the pledge against strong drink, I for one am prepared to do so."

He then pronounced the benediction, as had been arranged, and the little schoolhouse emptied itself in a twinkling.

Hugh was apparently his only convert!

. . . .

On reaching the door, Adam Clements told Willie Moynagh to go home by himself, for that he had an "arrand in another direction".

Willie started ostensibly for home, but turned shortly to dog Adam's footsteps, and watched him overtake and attach himself to two figures who were turning the first corner.

Mrs. Tuffit was very stout and walked slowly, and being a fluent conversationalist the first part of the journey that ended at her home passed pleasantly. After her chaperonage was removed, there remained a half mile to that of Martha, during which Adam racked his sluggish brain for some suitable remarks. He desired them to be of an intimate nature, but felt it impossible to evolve still less utter them. It was now a twelvemonth or more since he had begun to escort Martha from meetings, for the greater part of their progress tongue-tied, once the weather was animadverted on. The Temperance Meeting had been discussed in all its aspects during Mrs. Tuffit's presence, and Adam's contribution to the entertainment mentioned with many giggles from Martha, that fell like molten lead on her lover's heart. Poor Adam felt bitterly conscious that he had brought stain on his hitherto spotless character.

After walking by his sweeheart's side on the very narrow footpath for a quarter of a mile, an interesting bit of information inspired him.

"Did you hear that traycle's up?"

"D'ye tell me that?" said Martha excitedly.

"Oh, aye, traycle's quarely up." He endeavoured to amplify the precious theme.

"Man oh!" responded Martha.

They had now entered the lane that led to the cottage. Too soon they were at the door that had been left on the latch against Martha's return. Meetings were the only dissipation that came her way demanding late hours, for, as a Methodist's daughter, dances were prohibited.

No light shone from any window, and the house itself seemed asleep. On the doorstep Adam held Martha's solid hand in ecstatic silence as long as she permitted. "When will I see you again?" he entreated.

"When traycle's down!"

There was a swish of muslin skirts, and Adam at last realized that he was alone on the doorstep, underneath the bright stars.

CHAPTER XVI

THE TEA-PARTY

Is it a party in a parlour?
Crammed just as they were crammed,
But as you by their faces see
All silent and all damned. — WORDSWORTH.

OLIVER had written to Mrs. Hill requesting politely that he might bring the Rev. Hugh Noble, who had arrived unexpectedly, to her party, and Mrs. Hill had replied in gracious vein that it would give Dr. Hill and herself much pleasure to have the addition of Mr. Noble to their little party. (She failed to add that it would give her daughter Eleanor a great deal more.)

"I think we shall find him a satisfactory neighbour," the doctor had remarked after reading Oliver's note, which his wife had dutifully handed him. "I formed a good impression of him the day I called. He appears to have quite refined tastes, for he called my attention to the beautiful view from his windows. A young man," pronounced Dr. Hill, "who admires the beauties of nature is apt to be at heart a gentleman. But, of course, Miss Temple, you are well acquainted with him. I had for the moment forgotten that you were in some way connected. Am I not right?"

"Uncle Andrew (but, of course, he is only my uncle by marriage) is his mother's uncle, so, of course, Hugh is a second cousin of his. But I am nothing at all."

"You have met him, however?"

"Occasionally."

"And you also have a good opinion of him, I am sure?"

Hester blushed, and Nellie came to the rescue.

"Papa, Hester has a good opinion of everyone."

"That is an admirable characteristic to possess, and I hope Miss Temple's experience of life may justify her amiable attitude thereto."

. . . .

The drawing-room of 1st Bannerstown Manse seemed quite full when the two friends made their entrance, and the atmosphere fairly hot. The two windows were tightly closed, that being the era when "the night air" was regarded as a murderer ever on the alert for the unwary.

The ladies had been ushered up to Mrs. Hill's bedchamber, and had slid their wraps between the drawn curtains of her canopied four-poster. Being mere men and therefore not requiring a mirror to assist in the operation they simply hung their hats and coats on the already groaning hall-stand, assisted by Dr. Hill, who shone above all things in the capacity of host.

After this divestment he led them to the inner shrine and from chair to sofa and sofa to chair introducing—"our young brother Mr. Whiteside of Ballydaisy, and his friend Mr. Noble from a distance." The latter title substituted in lieu of Hugh's congregation, the name of which had escaped Dr. Hill's memory.

After a somewhat bewildering and giddy round, "Mr. Noble from a distance" found himself in a wedged position beside "my daughter Eleanor, whom I understand you have already met." That young lady having decreed that a sofa made to seat four should accommodate five, each of its occupants protesting that they had "loads of room".

For Oliver as he circled round, shaking hands, there was one face in the room that obliterated all the rest, and he arrived opposite it with his heart accelerated. "I need not introduce you to this lady," the doctor said facetiously, "she is, I understand, a thirty-second cousin," and he found a place for Oliver by her side.

They laughed at the doctor's wit. "You are Hugh's cousin and why not mine, too," he dared, "for Hugh and I are cousins."

"I always thought cousinship a nice relationship," she said, "not too near to quarrel."

"Then we're cousins. That's settled."

Meanwhile Eleanor and Hugh were having their own little dialogue.

"I'm sure you never remember seeing me before," said she.

"Distinctly."

"Where?"

"Often in May Street Church, and on one memorable occasion in Miss White's exclusive drawing-room."

"I got it for that. I'll never do it again. I saw you at Mr. Whiteside's ordination, but, of course, you didn't notice me."

"How do you know?"

Eleanor laughed and shook her curls. This was a frequent form of reply indulged in by her, and gave the impression that she had made a witty remark.

"I wonder what the name of your congregation is?" (She knew well.)

"Ballyswallow."

"You are the swallow?"

"They have to swallow me, I'm afraid."

At this stage Dr. Hill advanced to the frightened looking little bride in whose honour and Oliver's the party was projected, and crooked his arm at her, telling Oliver to kindly give his arm to Mrs. Hill.

The dining-table had been enlarged to meet the occasion by the addition of the hall-table. There was also a side-table at which sat Eleanor, Hugh, and the Rev. Benjamin Summers of Klergymore, who since Mr. Watson's recent adventure in matrimony, alone with Rev. Oliver Whiteside shared the bachelorhood of the Presbytery. Mr. Summers was the mildest of clerics, and dearly loved a tea-party. And although his fair hair was beginning to thin at the top, to sit at a side-table with Nellie Hill was his idea of earthly bliss.

Dr. Hill deftly carved the chickens, and, at the same time, led the conversation on high-minded matters, while the shy bride who was seated at his right hand instinctively turned to Oliver for refuge. Her host overawed her, but although this was the first time she had met Mr. Whiteside, she was very soon confiding to him what was her greatest concern—the shortcomings of the Manse, of which she had lately become mistress.

The parlour was so small you could hardly turn round in it. She didn't know what they would do in the winter when the fire was lit, they would have to push the table against the wall. The drawing-room was not quite so small, but so damp. James had got it papered for her, but the damp was beginning to come out in the walls again.

Oliver's ears were lent to the trials of the young housekeeper, but his eyes strayed across the table. He was feasting not on Mrs. Hill's tender chicken and succulent ham, but on a white brow curtained on each side by brown hair, and eyes "that were in their own selves a soul".

These heavenly orbs were at present serenely bent on Dr. Hill, who was declaiming thus:

"It is certainly more than a coincidence, that now our Church freed from the bane of Arianism[10] is at liberty to set herself to the great question of further advantages for ministerial training. That this magnificent legacy of Mrs. Magee[11] should fall into her lap at this auspicious time is above all things providential."

"It will all depend on how it is used," said the Rev. Samuel McConkey tartly. The acidity of his nature had certainly not been sweetened by a forty years' ministry in 2nd Bannerstown. He had been forced to watch that congregation dwindling slowly under the prestige of fashionable 1st Bannerstown. Mr.

---

[10] **Arianism**: The Arians, followers of the teachings of Arius (c. AD 250-336), believe that Jesus was created by and therefore subordinate to God and today are known as Unitarians. In the 1829 Subscription rift most of the break-away Remonstrant Synod were Arians.

[11] **Mrs. Magee:** Martha Maria Magee (c. 1755-1846), widow of Rev. William Magee, bequeathed £20,000 to the Presbyterian Church for the building of a college of theology and the arts. After much controversy it opened in Derry/Londonderry in 1865. It is today a campus of the Ulster University.

McConkey believed it was the music of the latter that did all the harm; for he credited the evil one with being the author of what was called "good music".

The highbrow topics discussed at the principal table were completely ignored at the side-table. Here Eleanor was in her element between Mr. Summers and Mr. Noble, encouraging each with a fine balance of justice, for her amiable system consisted of never discouraging any man who crossed her path to make love to her.

The ladies were not expected to contribute much to the conversation around the high table. Dr. Hill's stately periods were directed entirely to his brethren. Mrs. Hill was fully absorbed in filling and refilling the cups, assisted by the lady sitting next her. This was Mrs. Junk in her wedding dress of rich purple silk that could "stand alone". And no one, not even Dr. Hill in his most Pecksniffian[12] moments, could overawe Mrs. Junk. Two years ago she, being a widow, married of set purpose Rev. Titus Junk, of Windygap. So far apparently she had had everything her own way. Little Mr. Junk had just arrived at the determination that this state of affairs must end. Even now as he was sitting decorously attentive to Dr. Hill's fulminations, and agreeing—for he always agreed—with a deferential nod of his head, no one would have imagined that he was actually planning a *grand coup* to come off that very night for his wife's discomfiture. He was an exceedingly meek man, but it is the meek of the earth that astonish us one time or another.

---

[12] **Pecksniffian**: Seth Pecksniff is a sanctimonious character in Charles Dickens' novel *Martin Chuzzlewit*.

When everyone seemed to have drunk a third cup and "done", as their host would have said if it had been in anybody else's house, "ample justice to the viands set before them" (for most of them had driven more or less distances), the ladies retired to the drawing-room, while the menfolk lingered in the dining-room, for what purpose it is hard to say. One might as well have found fault with any of the theorems of the Westminster Confession of Faith as have proposed to light a pipe under the revered doctor's righteous roof-tree. The clergy of that day abjured the appearance of evil and held to high ideals of conduct, which gained for them the respect that has since decreased perceptibly.

The weakness of Mr. Summers for the ladies led him to glide stealthily after them, to be rewarded by Nellie Hill's devotion until such time as the other males came on the scene. When that time arrived there was no little difficulty in providing everyone with the means of sitting. This was at length accomplished more or less satisfactorily; their august host balancing himself carefully on a chair fetched from the backwater of the study, where it had been banished in disgrace from the drawing-room in order to prevent strangers who were ignorant of its peculiar infirmity patronizing it. Only its own family knew how to "humour" it. What it demanded was simply rigid uprightness; but presume on any familiarity with its back, and repentance followed sure enough—and that quickly.

Over the seated company hung that silence peculiar to evening parties, until Dr. Hill assumed the role of master of ceremonies by appealing:

"Eleanor, my dear, would you play us that beautiful piece, 'Home, Sweet Home'?"

There were few pianos then around Bannerstown, and Eleanor's very amateurish performance was the means of diffusing an innocent pride in her father's heart. After the proper demur Eleanor obliged. The white arms in the wide muslin sleeves crossed and recrossed in a manner marvellous to the uninitiated, as variation succeeded variation, obscuring the sweet melody, so that to find it was like putting a dissected map together. A murmur of conversation arose under cover of the music, at which Dr. Hill raised his hand with a smile and a polite "s-s-s-h". Finally the white arms pounced on a chord, were lifted in the air, and after a moment drooped to her lap. Then did the backwoods' conversationalists outrival all others in applause, and you could have lit a candle at the glow on the good doctor's face.

At last Oliver was sitting beside Hester, and when the embargo on conversation was lifted they talked of Oliver's new sphere.

"You'll have a busy time now making the acquaintance of all your congregation, and I know they have been accustomed to good visiting, for Mr. Brown and my uncle were great friends, and he used to come to see us at Taraghan. I remember him telling us that his servant-man, who was a Catholic, used to drive him, and he would often say to Mr. Brown. 'Dear! but you have oul' bother with your people!' "

Oliver laughed. "The same fate is in store for me, but I'll have to do it on Shanks's mare, for I could never rise to a 'conveyance'."

"No, I suppose not. It's a poor congregation Mr. Brown used to say; he was ashamed of having a bit of carpet on his sitting-room while they had earthen floors. He blamed the landlord very much, but I suppose he was no worse than the others."

"That's bad enough. I sometimes think if Dante had lived in our age he would have had a special circle for Irish landlords."

"You wouldn't think I was a descendant of theirs?"

"I often heard my mother say that Aunt Noble had come of 'county' people."

"Yes, her mother, who was my grandmother, belonged to a landlord family, and actually married a young Presbyterian minister who came to the neighbourhood. It was not supposed that she would ever meet socially such a person, but a broadminded gentleman near used to invite the young minister, and it was at his house my grandmother and grandfather met. Of course, her family were exceedingly displeased. I remember when we were children and grumbled about learning our catechism, my grandmother used to say, 'I had to learn mine after I was married.' Her daughter, Aunt Emily, married Uncle Noble, a Presbyterian minister, and her only son, who was my father, also became a Presbyterian minister."

"At any rate, you are 'a brand plucked from the burning'," said Oliver.

There was a stir in the room, a moving of seats and general re-arrangement. Mr. Summers was going to recite, and was taking his stand in a limited space that had been cleared for him.

He looked ingratiatingly at his audience, pushed

back the long fair lock that always lay on his forehead, cleared his throat, said he had a slight cold, was given a lozenge out of Mrs. Junk's purple silk pocket, hastily swallowed it, and began in a deep voice that seemed at variance with his pink and white complexion.

The poem chosen[13] represented a Vaudois merchant travelling through the land selling his wares, but having concealed in his pack Bibles, which when opportunity came to him he also offered.

"Oh! lady fair," he began, fixing his blue eyes on Eleanor, "these silks of mine are beautiful and rare—"

Dr. Hill settled himself for a treat. It was a favourite poem of his. With arms folded and eyes following every gesture of the dramatic Mr. Summers, he entirely lost himself in his enjoyment. His spirit, severed for the time from his beloved Bannerstown, soared high in the Alps, while his earthly body deprived of its control leant heavily against the back of his chair. Mrs. Hill prognosticating disaster made frantic attempts to catch the eye that saw nothing save "snow peaks keen".

Just as Mr. Summers was stealthily taking a Bible from his pack, and saying with intense meaning—"This, lady fair—"

On which Dr. Hill's chair quietly severed itself, and the back portion bearing the doctor's body began to disappear rapidly, before the onlookers realized that its velocity might have been checked with a little presence of mind.

[13] **poem chosen**: The poem is 'The Vaudois Teacher' by the American Quaker poet John Greenleaf Whittier (1807–1892).

But alas! that benevolent countenance, with its despairing appeal for help, vanished backwards and downwards, leaving in its place two large green slippers embroidered with red roses.

There was a shriek! Not from the doctor, who was strangely mute, but from the little bride whose absorbed gaze at Mr. Summers had prevented her noticing anything unusual in her surroundings, until the moment when she received Dr. Hill's revered head in her lap.

Mr. Summers hastily forsook the Albigenses and their Bibles, and as he was already on his feet rushed to give first aid, by attempting to reverse the doctor. All around joined to assist him in the effort, and everyone in the room pressed forward to inquire from Dr. Hill if he was hurt.

The episode was treated by Dr. and Mrs. Hill with due solemnity, and the cause of the disaster immediately dispatched to its former oblivion.

The guests, taking their cue from their host and hostess, had perforce also to adopt grave expressions. All at once from the visitors' point of view the evening had turned into a tremendous successful entertainment. When one has to fight fiercely to hide overwhelming amusement, and strangle laughter beneath a necessarily concerned countenance, then does the inner man arise in revelry, such as was deemed to have departed long ages ago. Oliver avoided Hugh's eye, and Hugh refrained from looking in the direction of Hester. Even the Rev. Samuel McConkey began to enjoy himself as he had not done for many a year, and the efforts of the little bride to stop her giggles at intervals, were of small avail. The starch was washed out of the evening, and guests hitherto strangers became lifelong friends. Dr. Hill's resumed dignity had lost its controlling spell.

Under the cover of the reanimated conversation Mrs. Hill slipped away, to return after a little followed by a maid bearing a large tray. Plates of apple pie and custard were handed round. If Mrs. Hill was proud of anything it was of her custards. She also professed to schedule the standard of other housekeepers by the consistency of their custards. There was a right one (that of Miss Hill's) and anything more or less was reprehensible.

The eating of these confections with which all select little parties in Bannerstown concluded proved a risky undertaking for the acknowledged bipeds. They drew their knees tightly together, and were forced to remain in this strained position until surrendering their plates with an inward thanksgiving for deliverance from mishaps.

At ten-thirty the evening was sanctified by "worship". All joined in singing the second paraphrase to the tune "French".

O God of Bethel by whose hand,
  Thy people still are fed,
Who through this weary pilgrimage,
  Hast all our fathers led.

Dr. Hill read the chapter that enjoins hospitality on bishops, and invited the Rev. McConkey to "lead in prayer". The Rev. Samuel was notably longwinded in that exercise even for his day, yet one of the company was actually sorry when the tardy "Amen" came. Closely wedged on his knees beside

Eleanor, Mr. Summers prayed devoutly with an arm around that neat waist, secure in the knowledge that such a good man as Dr. Hill would keep his eyes closed.

It was long after midnight when the household retired. Mrs. Hill, that outstanding housekeeper, superintended the washing of the last spoon. Eleanor's curlpapers pressed the pillow as she lay thinking of the evening. Presently she slipped out of bed, re-lit the candle and tiptoed to her father's study. She detached a certain blue book from its appointed shelf, and turned familiarly to the page that proclaims so accurately the stipends of ministers. It informed her that Ballyswallow stipend was thirty-eight pound six shillings, at which she sighed, restored the volume to its place and went back quickly to bed.

....

That proved to be a fateful night to more than one of Dr. Hill's guests.

The Rev. Titus Junk and Mrs. Junk were driving home as was their custom in their own "croydon". The direct route was past the old parish graveyard, where lay the mortal remains of Mrs. Junk's late husband. For two years Mr. Junk had listened to the incomparable virtues of this deceased gentleman. This in itself was trying enough, but a more exasperating performance, that had also gone on for the same time, had at last keyed his mildness into revolt.

This sinister graveyard seemed always to be on their way, no matter from whence they were returning, and Mrs. Junk required her present husband to draw rein on reaching it, so that she might pay a visit to her former one. On this night the moonlight shone through the ancient trees, displaying the many green nameless mounds interspersed by large flat stones that even in death proclaimed the social importance of those underneath. To-night Mr. Junk seemed to have forgotten where he was going and drove steadily on.

Mrs. Junk laid a heavy hand on his arm. "Do you not see where we are?" she demanded sharply.

"Oh!" replied Mr. Junk in as casual a way as he could command, "do you want to get out?" And he drew up.

Mrs. Junk scorned to answer, and clambered down from the croydon.

He watched her climb over the low wall, her large heavy figure looking gigantic in her driving muffles, as she stepped over intervening graves, and made a bee-line to that of the man whom Mr. Junk had never met in his life, but whom he hated with frenzy. He saw her drop on her knees beside the pretentious tombstone, and at that very instant he clicked his tongue against the roof of his mouth, giving at the same time a tug to the reins. Fanny, the pony, seemed also to be a fervid conspirator. She flung out her feet, and sped "as a bird to its mountain", which in her case was a comfortable stall.

....

Mr. Junk was the meekest of mortals. Nevertheless that was the last nocturnal visit his wife paid to the paragon that lay in Ardtree churchyard.

CHAPTER XVII

THE REVIVAL

Multitudes, multitudes in the valley of decision.

JOEL III. 14.

THAT obscure country Meeting-house was destined almost immediately after the Rev. Oliver Whiteside's ordination within its walls, to be the scene and centre of almost, if not altogether, miraculous happenings.

He had just settled to what he conceived to be the humdrum routine of a country minister's life, when a stupendous wave of religious awakening swept over the country, and reached high-water mark around Ballydaisy. The year of 1859 will be for ever memorable in the annals of Ulster Prebyterianism.

This Pentecostal revival brought in its train phases rarely if ever experienced before. Hundreds were "stricken", otherwise physically prostrated, and the sense of sinfulness was so acute, that bodily agony was undergone until such time as they realized their sins were forgiven.

That remarkable visitation of the Holy Spirit was believed to be the answer to earnest prayer offered up at the village of Connor in Co. Antrim. From there, where the manifestation began, it spread like a flame of cleansing fire—by what earthly means no one could tell—until men, women, and even children, succumbed before its power, were seized and, as it were, forcibly gathered into the Kingdom.

. . . .

It was a Sabbath day in June. The doors of Ballydaisy Meeting-house stood open to the air, and in the stillness you could hear the rustling of the leaves on the old trees that kept watch over the Green.

The church was filled. An indescribable feeling pervaded it. The faces uplifted to the young minister had a rapt expression of expectancy, as if seeking relief from inward strain.

In the Green, on this particular Sunday morning, the talk had not been of fair or market, of crops or herds, but of strange happenings that could not be understood, but which all felt were moving rapidly to affect themselves.

Oliver read the fifty-first Psalm, and his always impressive rendering of the sacred words seemed intensified, as to-day they fell on his listeners' ears with almost unearthly solemnity.

"Hide Thy Face from our iniquities, and blot out all our transgressions."

A shriek, and the sound of a falling body. Somebody was "stricken"!

Women wiped the perspiration from their faces with handkerchiefs, while men rose in their seats and sat down again in helplessness, as at a situation which had never confronted them before.

"Mercy! Mercy!"

Then they realized that Maria McVey a careless pleasure-seeking girl, was stricken.

She lay moaning and ejaculating at intervals:

"I am crushed by a weight. ... I cannot breathe ... my sins are smothering me."

The minister left the pulpit, and bent over her,

"Though your sins be as scarlet they shall be white as snow," he repeated.

She became somewhat quieter.

Abram Teggart and Archie Kilpatrick carried her out, and the church emptied itself into the Green.

"Let us pray."

The minister led in supplication for the poor mortal lying prone bewailing her sins, while her sobs punctuated his prayer.

Every head was uncovered, and every heart joined fervently in the petitions. An uneasy feeling of deep sinfulness attacked the listeners, and there was much heart-searching amongst them. At its conclusion the stricken one sat up, the tears streaming down her cheeks.

"Friends," said Oliver, "I will lay aside the sermon I had prepared, and will speak simply and plainly to you of the way of salvation.

"Jesus is without doubt standing in our midst to-day, saying, nay, beseeching, 'Come unto Me.' Take Him I implore you at His word. The Spirit is I know at this moment striving with many of you. Do not quench it, for that is the unpardonable sin; and He may leave you and never strive with you again. Close at once with your Saviour. Now—this very minute—is the accepted time. To-day is the day of salvation"—his voice broke with earnestness and emotion—"I beseech you harden not your hearts! ... Salvation is a free gift. All the heresies in the world have arisen from the idea that you have to earn it. Lay your sinfulness on the blessed Lamb of God—Yours, and yours, and yours," he pointed an accusing finger at them—"lay them at the foot of the Cross where they were atoned for, and they will never rise in judgment against you at the last day. Forsake them for ever and cleave to Christ. He will free you from their power. Put your hand in His outstretched one, and let Him lead you on. No one ever asked Him in vain, no, not even in the agony of His dying hour. It has yet to be said that anyone who sought Him was repulsed. Take Him and serve Him to the end. In so doing you will have difficulties to face, and obstacles to surmount, and temptations to overcome and sins to turn away from with loathing, for the powers of evil will beset you, and try to win you from your choice; but be not afraid, He will see you through—aye, to the very end—and when you come to the 'Valley of the shadow of death', which may not be very far from any of us, He will make it bright and safe and glorious for you. I do beseech you this very hour to render yourselves acceptable to God, which is your reasonable service."

When the recording angel reveals what is written, it will be found, that "this man and that man were born there," that Summer Sabbath day in Ballydaisy Meetinghouse Green. They joined tremulously in singing:

"All mine iniquities blot out,
Thy Face hide from my sin,
Create a clean heart, Lord renew
A right spirit me within."

How often during that marvellous year, did those words wing their flight to the very Throne, from Meeting-houses, and schoolhouses, and barns, and kitchens over Ulster!

Reluctantly the congregation dispersed. Some followed Oliver desiring a further word with him, so that it was late in the afternoon when he reached the Manse, and sat down to the dinner that Ann had endeavoured to keep warm. He tried, but could not eat. That evening he was to preach in Dunwhilly schoolhouse, three miles away. It would soon be time to start. He drank a cup of tea and set out.

As he walked, he seemed to realize God in everything around him, the pink wild roses in the hedge, the blue pageant of the sky, the scent of the newly-mown hay. What was nature but the revelation of its Maker. He had never experienced such a state of spiritual exaltation before. God was in him, and around him, and at his right hand. The mountains spread before his eyes spoke of His power and might, and Schiller's words occurred to him—"The God-head is nearer to us on a mountain-top." He felt that he himself had reached a spiritual mountain-top that very day, and that new glowing life had been generated, consecrating him in a fuller sense than ever before.

At a cross-roads a little group of people had gathered, who waited for him, as those of old time used to wait for the Master to pass by. He knew some of them to be members of the parish church. One of them stepped forward.

"Will Your Reverence please say a few words to us?"

Once more he told of God's Love, of Christ's Atonement, of the Power of the Holy Spirit, and besought them each to lay hold for themselves.

All uncovered as he prayed under the blue sky.

There was a shining light on the face of the man who had spoken. He grasped the minister's hand in thanks, but remained speechless.

Then a woman came forward and said to Oliver:

"I am his wife. For three days and three nights he has been like one demented. He took it all of a suddint last Thursday just about day-le-gone. Him an' James Brady were sittin' crackin' at the fireside, when Robert begins to pech, an' with that he throws hisself on the flure. 'Man dear!' sez James, 'is it the colic ails ye?' 'It is not, it is my sins,' sez he.

" 'Och man alive!' says James stoopin' an' catchin' his two hands that were clawin' the air, 'sthrive to get up; if sins would knock a body down shure we might all be in the shough!'

"But he aye kept turnin' an' twistin', an' we helped him into bed. But syne the wink o' sleep ever he got since, lyin' through the day when he should be up, an' pechin' an' groanin', an' swayin' hisself about, an' then stravagin about at night, when he should be in his bed."

"But I have got the peace of God now," interposed her husband, his face illumined as if with an unearthly light. "It come to me like a shot when the ministher was prayin'."

In another short prayer Oliver thanked God, and committed the awakened soul into His care and keeping.

"I'll go on with you to the meetin' at Drumwhilly," said the convert.

"You'll take your tay first," said his wife.

"I will not, I am only hungry and thirsty for the Bread of Life."

Others also of the little group said they would accompany the minister, and like Christian and Faithful on their pilgrimage there was "sweet discourse of all things that had happened to them".

Arrived at the schoolhouse, those gathered around the door shook the minister's hand in silence, and in silence he responded.

There was not an empty seat inside, many standing outside the open windows, straining their ears for fragments of prayer, or some sacred words that might float out to them. Many of those inside and around the walls had not heard a prayer for years. Women were present who had gradually dropped the habit of attending service either in "church" or "meeting". Children sat on their mothers' knees strangely quiet. In some cases, even these little ones drank in the Gospel and received the Lord Jesus into their hearts in their own childish way; and doubtless the Master as of old "took them up in his arms and blessed them".

Oliver sat long at the little desk, his head bowed in his hands. The Holy Spirit seemed to envelop the place. How long he sat thus he did not know, and no one noticed the unusual. He felt in the very Presence of the Most High, and as if he were undergoing a rebaptism. Thoughts of his ordination and its futile forms and ceremonies, simple though they were, sprang to his mind. And now in this small whitewashed schoolroom, clericalism and ecclesiasticism and every other "ism" that too often veils the seeker from the sought, simply were not.

Rising at length to his feet, he poured out his whole soul in supplication for himself and those around him.

That was the real ordination of the Rev. Oliver Whiteside.

CHAPTER XVIII

A PECULIAR CEREMONY

Within this awful volume lies
The mystery of mysteries.
—SCOTT.

AFTER a sleepless night Oliver found himself next morning weighed down beneath a load of depression. Such is our spiritual pilgrimage. One day on the mountain peak of rapture, the next deep down in the Valley of Humiliation. He even doubted his own soul, his own capacity to meet this divine crisis.

After a meagre breakfast he went out and paced the garden paths. Much troubled in mind, and scarcely conscious of what he was doing, he wandered out of the white gate and up the hills. His own Meeting-house, the scene of yesterday's astonishing manifestations, seemed to beckon him, and was drawing him to it for consolation and help in his present need.

He expected the gate to be locked, and intended climbing over the low wall at a convenient place—the regular recognized entrance for week-day visitors—but found it unnecessary thus to lower his clerical dignity, for the gate stood open, the padlock hanging by the chain.

He strolled up the short ascent, and just as he reached the Meeting-house door, a mat came whirling out of it almost smothering him in dust, and after the whirlwind rushed out Mary Bell, the sextoness, covered with remorse and confusion.

"Did it hit Your Reverence? Here gimme your kester an' I'll wipe the dust off it. Dear! but that was an unchancy happenin' raisin' such a stour, an' nearly blindin' you at your own Meeting-house dure."

Oliver hastened to reassure her that there was no harm done, "but I see," he said, "I need not come in, for you are busy, and can do without me."

"Come in surely an' welcome," invited Mary.

The inside air held very strongly a sacred mustiness that is a peculiarity of Meeting-houses—a real Presbyterian fust compounded of the used-up air of the many Sabbaths that have gathered congregations within the walls, blent with the mouldiness of decaying Bibles; all the ingredients thoroughly impregnated with dampness. This hallowed poison was carefully sealed up and preserved from Sabbath to Sabbath, save on the mornings when Mary Bell flung out her mats.

Mary kept the Meeting-house fairly clean, lit the inefficient stove on winter mornings, provided a glass of water for the preacher in the session-room, and finally covered the moth-eaten faded red cushions of the pulpit, when the minister vacated it and the audience had filed down the aisles, in a futile attempt to prevent them fading any more.

Between these "turns" she stood in the vestibule with an important official air, arrayed in an antiquated black bonnet and an equally ancient black shawl.

The late Mr. Brown was, of course, her standard. What Mr. Brown did, and what Mr. Brown said, were evidently inspired. "There's no Mr. Brown nowadays," was a favourite asseveration of hers.

Nevertheless she was willing and eager to take Mr. Brown's young successor to her heart, and mother and instruct him in Mr. Brown-like methods.

Before the service on Oliver's first Sabbath as ordained minister, she entered the session-room where he was sitting rather nervous and apprehensive, and presented him with a big round peppermint "to clear his throat", and urged him not to "be afraid to speak out, for there were two or three a bit hard o' hearin'." She also directed him to give the number of the psalm out twice over on this account, for that had been Mr. Brown's custom. "He had the people fair spoiled," she added.

To-day she followed him into the shrouded church, and endeavoured to make him feel that he was quite at liberty to visit it any day of the week.

"To tell you the truth," she said, "I'm right glad you come up this mornin', for I stan' in need of your advice about a sartin' thing. Take a look roun'," she said, waving her hand dramatically, "an' you'll see the sates all throughother with oul' Bibles with mebbe the backs off an' the leaves Dear knows where. Nobody wants them now, an' no matther how I redd up the place it does me no credit. I dursn't burn them, for that would be doin' what I was often told was a deadly sin, an' the boys might call me 'Burn the Bible'. What would you advise sir?"

The question somewhat puzzled Oliver, and the more he thought the less remedy he could propose, so he remained silent.

Mary was one of those who pretend to seek advice when they have planned the course of action they intend to take, so she waited no longer for the minister's solution of the peculiar biblical problem.

"I was lyin' last night in me bed," explained Mary, "an' couldn't close an eye thinkin' on the commotion that took place in the Meetin'-house yestherday, the likes of which I never seen afore, an' the sthir Maria McVey raised—an' Dear knows, if there's anybody needs religion it's her, for she's the right flype of a hussy an' has no gumption at all. I mind a story they used to tell about her gettin' a new bonnet with a red rosey in it, an' when the milliner axed her which side she would have the rosey at, sez she 'the side next the congregation'.

"I couldn't get her out o' me head at all till I begun to think of me dear Mr. Brown that's with the Lord—for that always puts me over—an' how he would have han'led yestherday, an' from that to the cleanin' o' the Meetin'-house the day, an' I wished I had a' asked him what to do with the oul' Bibles. An' then I slep' an' I dreamed we were buryin' Maria McVey in the Green with her coffin covered with Bibles, an' with that I woke, an' like a flash it come to me, straight from Mr. Brown I'm sartin', 'bury them! just bury them in the Green like Christens!' "

The idea commended itself to Oliver as a very admirable one.

"If you could get me a spade I will do it now," he said.

"I'll run home for me own spade, an' I'll not be a crack till I'm back again. Just Your Reverence sit down an' rest yourself. I'll bring you a creepie outside if you'd like to sit there."

But Oliver said he preferred to walk about.

Mary was certainly not long returning, considering that in addition to procuring the spade she had also changed into her professional uniform. She was going to assist the minister at a solemn ceremony which demanded appropriate garb.

From pew to pew the minister and the sextoness went collecting leaves and backs and backless portions of Bibles and psalm-books, that even in their tattered state were sacred, and carried all reverently outside.

Close by the wall of the Meeting-house Oliver digged a strange little grave after which Mary handed him book by book, while he arranged them tenderly in their last resting place.

Almost, he felt moved to offer up a prayer of gratitude to God for their blessed lives. And if the words did not arise on his lips, they were the meditation of his heart. Doubtless some of these poor pages had brought comfort to the sorrowful or perchance new hope to the faint and despairing. Perhaps a text read for the hundredth time in one of them may at last have flashed a meaning on the reader's mind, sufficient to irradiate all his future life here and prepare him for the one beyond. Someone certainly from these pages had sung "The Lord's my Shepherd", in a voice tremulous with love and old associations, or at Communion seasons they had declared their loyalty to their Redeemer in "I'll of Salvation take the cup". These decayed yet still precious remains had fulfilled their life-work, and deserved an honourable end.

A little robin hopped close and looked on with bright eyes interested in the movements of the spade, and as the minister smoothed the ground above a lark arose in the next field and soared upwards, pouring out its ecstatic pæan of praise to the Giver of that perfect day.

The minister and his colleague raised their heads and harkened to that amazing outburst of song. It seemed a fitting benediction to their hallowed task.

. . . .

Mary Bell took home the spade, once more changed her bonnet and shawl for secular cap and apron, and resumed her shaking of the mats.

Oliver walked down the hill musing on the peculiar rite in which he had just engaged. The dark spirit had lifted. The morning's occupation he felt had been sent to him by a compassionate Father who oft-times when we are downcast, prepares for us a welcome distraction that diverts and calms the mind.

Ann's washing had delayed the dinner, so he sought the garden, taking note of much which must immediately be done. He planned bright vistas for the future, for he had Rachel's love of flowers. "And I must get a dog," he resolved, "if one has a dog and a garden, and 'the peace that passeth all understanding' one has everything the world can give."

Then he reflected that man desires companionship nowhere more than in a garden, and that he had fixed his choice, and come what would it was unalterable.

CHAPTER XIX

THE GENERAL ASSEMBLY

And prove their doctrine orthodox,
By apostolic blows and knocks.
—SAMUEL BUTLER.

A YEAR had gone by since that ever-memorable Sabbath day on which the Revival "broke out" around Ballydaisy. All that summer it continued unchecked. Meetings were held in the church, in schoolhouses, in barns and kitchens, and often on the public roads. People working in the fields ceased when they caught sight of the minister, gathered round him and implored a repetition of the Gospel message.

Many professed a change of heart and witnessed to it faithfully to the end of their lives. Others fell away. Yet the '59 Revival left a spiritual seal on Ulster that has not yet been broken. Its fruits were for eternity.

Thus was Oliver's first year in the ministry an abounding one. He thanked God for it, and gave himself body and soul to the work. Tired in body and exhausted in mind he felt at times, but later on when rested and refreshed he felt constrained to say, "He restoreth my soul".

Hugh paid him a visit in the autumn, and again in the spring. Oliver often said to him he did not know whether it was he or Eleanor Hill was the attraction, and Hugh would reply that he didn't know himself. Once Oliver returned the courtesy, and spent a week with Hugh at Ballyswallow. There was no doubt in that case of an incentive, for Ballyswallow was within driving distance of Hugh's home, Emerald Hill, which place, thought Oliver, contained a treasure far above its name. Hester Temple, left early an orphan, had been adopted by the Rev. Andrew Noble and his wife whose niece she was. Since leaving Miss White's select establishment she had lived a pleasantly busy existence composed of many different duties. Mrs. Noble had gradually passed into a semi-invalid, and willingly allowed her niece to take charge of the house-keeping while she enjoyed herself as a chastened and afflicted servant of the Lord.

In the church also Hester was her uncle's right hand. She led the singing after the death of the old precentor, gathering round her some of the younger members to form a choir; but her heart lay in the Sabbath school, for she loved children. And to the homes of the sick she came, bearing some little delicacy. Miss Hester's pot of jam was always to be counted on. So that going minus this offering one day to see an old bedridden exacting female, the defrauded one said inquiringly as Hester was taking her leave, "I suppose the jam's all done."

The oftener Oliver saw her the more deeply her image became graven on his heart, and if he was impatiently looking forward to the meeting of the General Assembly, it was not altogether from a profound interest in its ecclesiastical proceedings, but because he had heard Hester once say that she was going.

....

The "Assembly" was now over, and the "Fathers and Brethren" back to their spheres of work much refreshed in spirit from a renewal of old friendships, and from contact with fellow-labourers in the same field. Discouraged they might be, at what seemed to them the meagre results arising from their preaching, visiting, training the young, comforting the mourners, and advising the perplexed, all the time conscious of an isolation in remote country districts. All hardships, however, were forgotten when on the opening night of the Assembly in crowded "May Street", the Fathers and Brethren joined, some with more heart than voice, but all thrilled with one common feeling of pride in singing:

"Pray that Jerusalem may have
Peace and felicity,
Let them that love thee and thy peace
Have still prosperity."

They sang it to St. Paul's, and they maybe dragged out the tune more or less, for in those pure days no man-made instrument dare presume to aid in the worship of a pure God, and an organ dare no more occupy a position within four Presbyterian walls than a confession-box.

True, in a few congregations here and there, a small harmonium led the children's praise in Sabbath School—a concession to juvenility—but before twelve o'clock struck their lids were severely closed down, at which orthodox time the serious worship of the Almighty commenced.

This doubtful innovation had crept into fashionable First Bannerstown Sabbath School, amid some disapproval from the elder folk. One old elder, the treasurer of the congregation, would not after the service even empty the contents of the collecting-boxes on its convenient lid to count, but poured their coppers forth on the seat behind it, and bent his long old back to the task.

In the years to come "Pray that Jerusalem may have peace and felicity", was often to be the prelude within those May Street walls to fierce battles on "The Instrumental Music Question". One in particular, an outstanding combat, lasted till the small hours of the morning engaged in by a seething mass of frenzied enthusiasm. Of that historic scene the Rev. Oliver Whiteside was to be a witness and a participator.

On the opening evening of the Assembly Oliver stood on the steps of May Street exchanging greetings with old college friends while awaiting Hugh.

Yes, there he was at last! his tall hat at a slightly unclerical angle, as he took the steps two or three at a time with the old boyish zest. Behind with graver decorum came his father accompanied by a minister unknown to Oliver, and between them—how quickly his heart beat—walked Hester Temple. Then an incomprehensible emotion which he had never experienced before took possession of him.

Nevertheless there were warm shake-hands, after which he heard himself being introduced to the Rev. Obadiah Shimmens, who obligingly said he had frequently heard Hugh speak of Mr. Whiteside. Oliver made inquiries as to Mrs. Noble's health. She was much as usual. Next the weather was highly commended, Mr. Shimmens remarking that it invariably "took-up" for the Assembly.

The Rev. Obadiah was a very tall man and very thin, uncertain as to age, but certain as to ugliness—at least, so Oliver sized him up. His long jaws were clothed with whitey-brown whiskers, and his less abundant locks showing even more white than brown, were carefully combed over a desert on his crown. He bore the unmistakable stamp of the bachelor-minister, and carried Miss Temple's wrap over his arm.

Ministers accompanied by wives, daughters, and other lady friends were thronging in; and Mr. Noble saying they had better take their seats, led at once the way inside. Hester followed her uncle, and Mr. Shimmens followed Hester. In the pew selected there was only room for three, so that Oliver and Hugh were forced to occupy the one behind.

Never in his life had Oliver hated any man as he did this specimen immediately in front of him. To do him justice he tried to overcome this antipathy and to follow the proceedings conscientiously.

There was an exceedingly long and deeply-reasoned sermon by the outgoing Moderator, during which the Rev. Andrew Noble sat entranced, for that was his idea of entertainment. Hugh fidgeted in the seat behind, and Oliver, try as he would, could not follow the thread of the discourse. Raising his eyes decorously to the pulpit, next moment he would find them fastened on the brown hair covered by a net, the "drawn" silk fawn bonnet, and the sloping shoulders in the fawn pelisse. Contrariwise, he observed that the face beneath the silk bonnet never wavered from the intellectual visage of the Rev. Dr. Diggan, as he expounded his tedious "heads". Earthy substances, such as himself or even the fortunate Mr. Shimmens, did not at present evidently exist for Miss Temple. Once Hugh whispered a desire that the learned doctor would come to the tail, but when finally that appendage was reached, there still remained to be delivered his out-going address. After this correspondingly lengthy performance, there occurred the selection of a "new Moderator", and according to custom the chosen one was required to give a specimen of his competency for the exalted position by an "incoming address".

The male listeners trying to appear as though they were enjoying these heavy items, mopped their faces with large white handkerchiefs, the ladies fanning themselves delicately with their smaller ones.

It was long past "elders' hours" ere the "Fathers and Brethren" emerged into the delicious sweetness of an early summer night. Oliver, he knew not how, found himself walking along May Street by Miss Temple's side, while in the rear came the Rev. Shimmens with her uncle and cousin. Was it possible that the demure hanger-on on the Rev. Dr. Diggan's lips had accomplished this manœuvre? At any rate Oliver felt that Mr. Shimmens was even now of a surety returning in full measure his own brotherly feelings.

Hester and her uncle were staying in the Donegall Pass, which had now become a select suburb of Belfast. Oliver wished their destination ten times farther from May Street, for alas! it was reached in an incredibly short space of time, perhaps owing to their interesting discussion on Dr. Diggan's oratory, and the questions touched on in the "in-coming

Moderator's" speech. However, here they were on the doorstep, and Mr. Noble, tired from his journey that day but still more exhausted from the strain of listening for hours in the stifling atmosphere of "May Street", hastened ruthlessly to say "good night". Hester gave her hand to the three brethren in turn, two of whom, truth compels the avowal, gave it a surreptitious squeeze, of which she seemed not to be cognizant, for she followed her uncle quickly into the house, without once looking back.

Mr. Shimmens's way lay in the opposite direction to that of Oliver and Hugh. They had taken their old room at Mrs. MacBeth's for the Assembly, and they now strode across the "Chapel Fields" in a straight line for Hamilton Street.

Sad changes had Time brought there! The laughter-loving Kate of the golden-red mane and apple blossom cheek, now lay beneath the dank grasses of the Shankhill graveyard. Notwithstanding her mother's opposition, she had married her lover, but indeed any other choice of hers would have met with similar resistance, for of marriage in the abstract Mrs. MacBeth totally disapproved. Man, according to her, was a combination of treachery and turpitude, while presenting a front of plausibility to a world of poor gulled womanhood.

"You never know them till you're tied to them, they're that polished aforehand, but them that has a man has a masther." The late Mr. MacBeth surely felt amused and complimented to hear himself described in the latter capacity!

Pretty Kate, in spite of incessant direful warnings, took the risk of marriage gaily. What her eventual experience might have proved had time given a chance we may not know. For one short year of life happiness certainly was her lot, entrancing happiness with the birth of her baby girl. Perhaps she was envied of the gods, as the ancients believed. For in the awful cholera year that claimed such a toll of victims in Belfast, but a few hours' sickness, and the gay little lover of life was summoned to leave it. Yet even as she had done in this world, she carried bliss into the Beyond with her, for in her coffin lay her baby on her breast.

Kate's father had also ended a life that had never awakened in him much care or responsibility. Her husband and daughter had furnished Mrs. MacBeth with perennial material for cheerless lament. She had now the gratification of describing herself "a lone widda woman".

....

It was with a serious visage she greeted her two former lodgers, the grievance to-night proving to be that she had to sit up for them. But, as of old, the shining kitchen, the dazzling tins and brasses, and the table set with snowy cloth for their supper welcomed them.

"I'm afraid we're rather late," said Hugh.

"Oh aye!" she agreed, "them that follows religious meetin's never takes thought for them that's sittin' up at home. All my life I seen the converted ones runnin' here an' there till meetin's an' leavin' them that liked to get their fill of the work at home."

She poured out two plates of porridge from the saucepan, and placed two bowls of milk on the table.

Then she put on her spectacles and scrutinized her guests.

"You're both failed."

"Hard work," accounted Hugh.

"How are you yourself?" inquired Oliver.

"Oh, I'm just hingin' together," she sighed.

"Do you still take in students?"

"I just kep' one last winther. I'm not a match for more now. He was a great studier, an' sat up burnin' light an' fire on me. If it's not one thing they do on me it's another. I could have more, for I hear there's a dale of students at the college, an' more comin' forrard than there's any call for."

"There are very many more men than there are vacancies for," said Oliver.

"Well," said Mrs. MacBeth, "they'll just have to turn their attention to somethin' useful. What are you laughin' at, Mr. Noble? How does your people take with so much laughin'?"

"You know Mrs. MacBeth, we are told there is a time to laugh," apologized Hugh.

"Well, that time never come to me. Even when I was a young slip of a girl I was sayrious-minded, an' when I did go outbye I liked best to take a dandher in Mullaghadivity graveyard, an' read the descriptions on the stones, for the Reverend McSpadden aye kept warnin' us about our latter end. Did I ever tell you about one night he was sent for to go to see a wicked man that was dyin', an' as he was goin', sez he till the neighbour man that come for him, 'Is he afraid to meet his God?' An' sez the man, 'No, Your Reverence, it's the oul' boy he's afeard o' meetin'.' "

Oliver and Hugh knew they were intended to be

solemnly impressed by this narrative, and did their best to look it.

Mrs. MacBeth handed Oliver a candlestick. "You'll more nor likely not be up afore nine o'clock," she said, "but I never was one to lie in bed in the mornin's."

"We know well that you considered that a mortal sin," said Hugh.

"Aye an' it's the mortyal sin that ministhers is prone to—that's them that's goin' now," she qualified; "but I mind the Reverend McSpadden startin' out an' ketchin' his hearers at their breakfast."

"Fearful," commented Hugh, "enough to give them indigestion!"

"G'wan now, Mr. Noble, an' don't be wastin' your kennel, an' you Mr. Whiteside see that he puts it out an' doesn't burn us all in our beds."

CHAPTER XX

THE ASSEMBLY

Love rules the court the camp the grove,
And men below, and saints above.

—SCOTT.

DR. HILL and his daughter were also "up for the Assembly", and were staying with two maiden sisters originally from Bannerstown. These ladies lived just outside the town in Packenham Place, and kept their own cow which grazed in the field behind that was bordered by the muddy Blackstaff river. Wishing to make the acquaintance of the young minister of Ballydaisy which was in their former neighbourhood, they commissioned Dr. Hill to invite Oliver to tea with them. They were exceedingly prim paragons, and after tea Eleanor manœuvred Oliver to a distance in the drawing-room, and confided to him her misery. "If I had to stay another week with them," she said, "I would throw myself into the Blackstaff."

"Do it," he said, "when the brethren are coming up the Dublin Road, so that one of them may have the honour of rescuing you. Hugh is a capital swimmer."

"I saw him and Hester with you on the opening night. Poor me—I was in durance vile between these two dragons."

"I suggest we have a walk by the Blackstaff now," he said.

"Well, suggest it yourself to the Misses Herring if you want to see them faint."

Just then Dr. Hill arose, and "hoped his kind hostesses would have the goodness to excuse him, as he wished to hear the debate that evening, and possibly to participate in it."

Eleanor overjoyed sprang to her feet, and assured the Misses Herring that she, too, was immensely interested in that particular debate. The Misses Herring begged to be excused accompanying them, as they had paid some visits in the afternoon and were somewhat fatigued. Of course, they proffered, had not Dr. Hill been with Eleanor, one of them would certainly have accompanied his daughter. Miss Hill thereupon put out her tongue at the Rev. Oliver Whiteside behind the virtuous backs of Dr. Hill and the two ladies.

When they arrived at the steps of "May Street", Eleanor whispered to Oliver to look inside and see if Hester were there yet, a commission he accepted with singular alacrity, knowing at the same time that it was not altogether Miss Temple's society that her dear friend so much desired.

On the top-most step stood the Rev. Obadiah Shimmens looking over the heads of everyone, his countenance portraying pleasurable anticipation. Next moment Oliver saw him raise his tall hat very gallantly, while Miss Temple put her small hand into his large skinny one. It made severe demands on the younger minister's composure to be a witness of these ordinary courtesies.

The jade Fortune, as she often does at the worst, unexpectedly turns and smiles; for while Mr. Shimmens was, out of politeness, of which he had a superfluity, greeting the young lady's uncle,

Oliver gained Hester's side vowing that no one but himself would possess her that evening. Eleanor, who had wished so much to see Hester, did not seem so satisfied as one would have imagined, but kept looking round on all sides and watching those who were coming up the steps. Notwithstanding this restiveness on Miss Hill's part, Oliver made a move forward, Hester followed him and Eleanor could linger no longer, unless she coveted the Rev. Obadiah's company.

As they entered, the Assembly was on its feet singing:

"Behold how good a thing it is,
And how becoming well,
Together such as brethren are
In unity to dwell."

Under cover of this diversion the wily young minister of Ballydaisy ushered his two lady friends into a seat that had only room for three, leaving the forsaken Mr. Shimmens perforce to go forward with Uncle Noble "within the barrier".

Many brethren with young lady friends occupied the back pews, paying little attention to the platform speeches, so engrossed were they in their own. Nellie's gaze wandered over these seats, and at last detected the Rev. Hugh Noble sitting beside a very young and very pretty girl. Awarding him a curt nod, she calmly surveyed her field for future action.

Beside her sat a genial-looking spectacled specimen, who at intervals glanced sideways at her with evident admiration. Nellie dropped her reticule (shades of Miss White!). Spectacles hastened to restore it with a twinkle of his glasses and, of course, it was but polite to thank him. After doing so, she became apparently very much interested in the speech that was being delivered, and when it was finished modestly asked her neighbour if he would kindly inform her who the speaker was. Spectacles beamed and replied that it was the Rev. Jeremy Sturrock of Ballydeuteronomy—"fine delivery," he added, "don't you think so?" and Nellie was, of course, obliged to give her opinion. Naturally they felt inclined to criticize the speakers that followed, so that at the end of the sederunt Miss Hill was satisfied that her evening had not been entirely wasted.

After the benediction was pronounced, she had out of politeness to say "good night. I expect," she added graciously, "you are looking for your wife now?"

Spectacles replied smilingly and with emphasis, "I am, and I'm looking this long time for her."

"I do hope you'll find her soon," said Nellie, presenting him with a shake of her curls and her sweetest smile, as she left him to follow Hester and her escort down the aisle.

In the hall they waited to give Nellie into her father's charge, and to find Uncle Noble, who kindly told them to walk on and he would overtake them, as he wished to speak with Mr. Shimmens about an exchange for Sabbath.

Once more Oliver had the overwhelming satisfaction of walking to "the Pass" by Hester's side. Alas! the way seemed even shorter than the previous night. His pleasure was considerably lessened, however, when on the way Miss Temple informed him that she and Uncle Andrew were going home next day – they had been long enough away from Aunt Emily, and intended starting for Emerald Hill in the morning.

"I believe I'll go home in the morning, too," Oliver said.

"Oh! why would you do that, you'd miss the great debate on Friday night."

"I don't care," said the Rev. Oliver Whiteside.

She was shocked!

How much he wanted to say, while every step was mercilessly taking the possibility of uttering it farther away. Now they were actually in "the Pass", and his dejection became deeper. All of a sudden it vanished as Hester remarked – "Maybe you'll come with Hugh to our visitation."

"When is it?" he said eagerly.

"The first Tuesday of October."

"I wish it was Tuesday first."

"Then you'll come?"

"If alive."

They were now at the door, and Mr. Noble hurrying up joined them.

"Wasn't it a fine debate?"

"Splendid," said Oliver.

"Could you hear it well? You were very far back."

"Perfectly," said Oliver.

"I thought Dr. Cook surpassed himself."

"So did I."

"Well, good-bye, Oliver. Hester and I must return to-morrow, but you and Hugh, I suppose, will see the matter out."

"Oliver intends to come to our visitation at Taraghan," interposed his niece.

"Yes, indeed, it might interest him to meet the brethren of the Uphill Presbytery."

"Thank you very much, Uncle," he said with unfeigned gratitude, "I would certainly like to go."

He held Hester's hand as long as he dared, and then turned to Hamilton Street with a firm, happy step.

It was a good half-hour before Hugh turned up. Oliver began to upbraid him for deserting them at the Assembly. "I saw you in the back seat with a young lady. Who was she, anyway? You seem to know them all."

"A few," admitted Hugh. "This particular one was Fanny Sturrock, old Sturrock of Ballydeuteronomy's daughter. She's better worth listening to than he is."

"We'll have to find him a sensible girl, and get him to settle down, Mrs. MacBeth," said Oliver.

"Is it sense you're lookin' for in the girls goin' nowadays?" exclaimed Mrs. MacBeth. "Shure you might as well look for holy wather in an Orange Lodge!"

"Aye, and ministers' daughters have the least sense of all," said Hugh.

Mrs. MacBeth sighed. "Has it come to that! In my young days, they were just examples to the congregation. The Rev. McSpadden's daughter now was born good. She had the Bible read through, an' a patchwork quilt made, afore she was eight years old."

"I wonder what it's like to be born good," remarked Hugh.

"Aye, it must be an unusual sensation," said Oliver.

"Yous two has more breath than sense," reproved Mrs. MacBeth.

CHAPTER XXI

THE EMERALD HILL HOUSEHOLD

Honest labour bears a lovely face.
—DEKKER.

IT was tea-time at Emerald Hill. The Rev. Andrew Noble and Hester Temple sat at the square table, while Mrs. Noble sat on the corner of the couch nearest the fire, for she had played the role of invalid more or less for the greater part of her life. Her mother, a woman of unbounded energetic temperament, had brought her up to believe she was delicate, and the amiable girl acquiesced agreeably.

From childhood Emily Temple had manifested strong spiritual tendencies. This, combined with beauty and delicacy, appealed to the robust young minister of Taraghan. He married her, and took up the nursing where her mother had left off.

"We are to have Mr. Shimmens to announce the visitation next Sabbath," said the minister.

"Who?" said his wife. She was somewhat deaf, but insisted on the repetition of a remark until she heard it; an exaction that sometimes irritated her husband, when, perhaps, he had to reiterate some trivial utterance, and Mrs. Noble herself on grasping it showed her disgust at its unimportance.

"I said Mr. Shimmens, Mister-Shim-mens, and there is no one for whom I have a greater regard," he added. "I believe he is untiring in visitation among his people."

"What did you say about him?"

"I merely said he was a good visitor."

"That's only the right and proper thing in a minister," said Mrs. Noble, "but I'm told that nowadays many of the younger men neglect that duty. Dr. Morgan sets them a fine example in that."

"I would hardly include Mr. Shimmens in the category of the younger men," said Hester smiling. "He's fifty if he's a day."

"Did you say he was sixty, Hester?"

"No, Aunt Emily, I was merciful and only said fifty."

The Rev. Andrew looked severely at his niece. "Mr. Shimmens is in the prime of life, and at the summit of his power," he said.

Hester rose hastily to take her aunt's cup. "Won't you have a little less sugar and a little more cream, and not quite so strong."

"I'll get some more hot water," said Hester, picking up the jug.

"If you are going to the kitchen," said her uncle, "tell Isaac to come and speak to me after tea."

A little later the parlour door was unceremoniously opened without any preliminaries and a figure appeared in the doorway. It was that of a man no longer very young, not very tall, but broad-shouldered and squarefaced clad in a "sleeved weskit" and corduroy trousers, with garters of twine under each knee.

This was Isaac the servant-man, who had come as a lad to Emerald Hill when the minister acquired the small farm and dwelling, and had set up his household there shortly after his ordination. As the years advanced it was difficult to say which was master and which man. The Rev. Andrew still assumed that he was master, and issued commands, which if Isaac considered were for the good of "the place", he had no objection in carrying out. If otherwise he refused to obey them.

Mrs. Noble clutched her shawls and drew them close around her. "Please come in, Isaac, and shut the door," she said. Then she held her handkerchief delicately to her nose, for Isaac carried with him invariably the aroma of the stable and the byre.

Isaac smiled indulgently at her, and gave the door a push with his foot. He always admitted that he "humoured the mistress".

"Isaac," said his master, "the Presbytery meets for visitation in Taraghan on Tuesday of next week. The walks around the Meeting-house will require to be scuffled, and the grass in the Green cut. You must find time to clip the hedges also. Nothing gives such a neat appearance as well-trimmed hedges."

"Oh! many's the time I've scuffled the walks and cut the hedges for *them,* afore," said Isaac gloomily.

"Yes," said the minister, "they have always complimented us on the neatness of our property."

"So well they might," said Isaac complacently. "It's me that knows that! But it's gettin' near-han' the time that the pirdas was dug out."

"The potatoes must wait," said his master firmly.

"Well, I'll see what I can do," said Isaac agreeably.

"And Isaac," continued his master, "when you are in town to-morrow for the yellow meal get me a tin of green paint for the Meeting-house gate. I'll give you the money for it, now," said the minister taking out his purse.

"It's a clane jab they put you to," said Isaac sarcastically, "why a weddin' would come aisyer on us than that visytation. But if I've time I'll scuffle the walks for them anyway," he conceded, and retired to the kitchen, where he seated himself on a creepie and sighed heavily.

"Have they finished their tay inside?" inquired Nancy. "I want to get redd up."

"You know little of reddin' up, if you had to redd up the Meeting-house Green for the visytation comin' roun', you might talk; why the very graves has to be put in ordher to satisfy them, an' here's the masther takin' it on hisself to pent the gate again. 'Get me a tin o' green pent,' sez he, 'when you're in the town the morra'—takin' the money out of his own pocket."

"Och oh! d'ye tell me that!" exclaimed Nancy. "Such a han' as he makes of himself! The last time he come in with his very baird green! An' he won't wear an apern."

"I'm just afther tellin' him an' her that a weddin' wouldn't put us more about."

"Take care but you might have that same on your han's soon too." With this dark saying Nancy took her tray and disappeared.

Isaac pondered deeply in her absence, and by the time she was back with the cups and saucers he was ready for her.

"Is it yourself at long last, an' thon oul' widda man that's been puttin' spake on ye this ten year?"

It was common knowledge that Nancy had "a good bit o' money" past her in the Savings Bank, and suitors were not wanting. She began washing up the dishes in her usual deliberate manner, soliloquizing at the same time for Isaac's benefit: "We were foolish to think we could keep her, barrin' we locked her up where no man could set eyes on her."

The light suddenly penetrated to Isaac's brain. "Which o' thon ministhers is it? Is it the long ribey one over beyant? He has a good many nicks in his horn!"

"They'd be ill off that'd take him," said Nancy scornfully.

"'Deed I wouldn't take him meself," agreed Isaac.

"Mebbe it's thon tarrible well-set-up one with shoulders like a prize-fighter, that comes wi' Masther Hugh?"

"I wouldn't say but it might," admitted Nancy.

"Boys oh!" exclaimed Isaac. Then realizing that he had allowed himself to be betrayed into a profitless conversation he said, "Just look at ye keepin' me here with your blethers in place of out-bye foddherin' the kettle. You weemen's nothin' but geb, geb, geb!" And with as much clatter of the creepie as he could produce, he stamped to the door.

CHAPTER XXII

THE REV. OBADIAH SHIMMENS

It were all one
That I should love a bright particular star
And think to wed it.

—SHAKESPEARE.

IT was a warm Sabbath afternoon. At morning service Mr. Shimmens had preached in Taraghan from the text: "Behold thou art fair my love, behold thou art fair, thou hast dove's eyes", and afterwards announced the "visitation". Now, he and Miss Temple were sitting in the drawing-room, his face beaming with satisfaction, hers filled with dismay at the prospect of a protracted *tête á tête* with her elderly admirer.

It was Mrs. Noble's custom to spend Sabbath afternoons on her sofa in the cosy little parlour, in company with a volume of the Rev. Murray McCheyne's sermons, over which she luxuriantly dozed; all the time conscious of a sanctified feeling that its contact imparted. Hugh irreverently described his mother's habit as "The Saint's Everlasting Rest".

From any form of literature that professed to portray the joys and sorrows of our common life Mrs. Noble religiously averted her eyes. The newspaper she also excluded, and she was continually surprised at the avidity with which her husband followed the political machinery of the British Empire. He, on occasions, wishing to rouse her out of herself and interest her in mundane surroundings, would suggest that she should take a look at the *Northern Whig,* whereupon she would gravely and incontrovertibly reply: "Andrew, at the last day I shall not be asked if I read the *Northern Whig.*"

So, while Mrs. Noble slumbered peacefully in one room, it fell to her niece's lot, in the other, to tackle the entertaining of the divines who occasionally exchanged pulpits with her uncle.

To-day's duty was particularly uninviting, yet she found herself talking at a greater rate than ever before, while her eyes looked out longingly on the green lawn, and the inviting seat beneath the "weeping willow", that only permitted the bold sun to take a peep here and there at its shielded guest. How many hours since childhood had she and Hugh spent in that enchanted spot with faithful friends, of whom Sir Walter Scott and Charles Dickens were the chief, and for delightful companion on Sabbath afternoons, John Bunyan. Hugh indeed showed a partiality for Captain Marryat and Baron Munchausen, to Mrs. Noble's manifest distress of mind. One day when her aunt required a little "fine sewing" done, she had found her precocious niece absorbed in *Nicholas Nickleby,* and had solemnly warned her that such an occupation was not a very good "preparation for the world to come". That young lady's retort almost stunned her:

"I would rather meet Charles Dickens in heaven than Abraham, Isaac, and Jacob!"

This train of thought supplied by contemplating the "weeping willow", suggested a safe subject of conversation with her guest.

"Our old friend Mayne Reid is getting famous," she said. "Many a game Hugh and I and he had together, although he was much older."

"He was a mischievous boy, I'm afraid," said Mr. Shimmens, "rumours of his pranks still remain in the neighbourhood."

"I remember," said Hester, "his father once sending him to ask for an old woman in the congregation who was very ill. Mayne mounted his donkey and set off. Arrived at the door of the cottage and seeing no one within, he rode his donkey across the kitchen floor into the room beyond, and only drew rein beside the bed. The clatter awoke the old creature, who, opening her eyes suddenly, saw the great ears of the donkey, and began to shriek, believing it was his Satanic Majesty come to take her away bodily. How Mayne enjoyed that escapade!"

"I believe his mother intended him to follow in his father's footsteps and be a minister," said Mr. Shimmens.

"Yes," said Hester, "and although he is now so famous, she is not yet reconciled. He said himself recently that his mother would rather have seen him in the poorest Ulster Presbyterian pulpit than Prime Minister of England."

Then the conversation turned on "calls" and "ordinations", and "installations", and such appropriate functions fitted for the sacred day. All the while Hester keeping watch on the clock on the mantelpiece, listened eagerly for the wheels of her uncle's chariot which would herald deliverance.

"Perhaps you would like to read a little now, Mr.

Shimmens," she said at length, feeling somewhat exhausted. "Here is the last number of the *Evangelical Witness*. It is a most interesting one."

"I am certain it is, Miss Hester, but not nearly so interesting to me as yourself!"

This was ominous, and she plunged wildly: "Isaac pretends to be very much annoyed about the visitation," she said.

"He seems a curious fellow," remarked Mr. Shimmens.

"Oh! he's a character, but entirely devoted to 'the place'."

"Last time," said Mr. Shimmens, "that I had the pleasure of being here, we were chatting as he drove me home, and he referred to 'my wife'. I informed him I was unmarried. He looked at me with evident surprise, and said: 'I wonder greatly at that, for you're very entisin'.' "

Hester's laugh was sincere.

"I wish someone would find me 'entisin'', Miss Hester," and drawing his chair closer she saw a long arm extending, evidently with the intent to encircle her neck. So great was her horror it might have been a boa-constrictor. Never had she found her feet so quickly.

Next instant a sound sweeter than music fell on her ears.

"Why, there is uncle already," she exclaimed, "you will have to excuse me, he demands his tea immediately he comes in. Dear Uncle Andrew is a most impatient person." She fled for refuge to Nancy and the tea kettle.

....

That evening after supper, and the departure of Mr. Shimmens, the Rev. Andrew Noble looked several times earnestly at his niece as though regarding her in a new light. Finally he addressed her.

"Hester, my dear, Mr. Shimmens has spoken more than once to me about you."

"About me, Uncle! What can he have to say about me? I know I'm not just sound on the instrumental question, but he cannot excommunicate me for that!"

"Hester, be a little less flippant, please. Mr. Shimmens is desirous of having you for his wife. He has formed a very high opinion of your worth, and I have persuaded Mamma that it would be entirely suitable. Isn't that your opinion, Mamma?"

"I'm told he has a beautiful Manse," urged Mrs. Noble feebly.

"And so dear Uncle and Aunt, you consider it would be a good 'sittingdown'."

"Far from it, Hester, Mr. Shimmens is a man of sterling rectitude and unblemished character."

"But I couldn't marry sterling rectitude any more than I could a Manse. If ever I want to marry, I'll marry a man."

"And what pray do you call Mr. Shimmens?"

"A fossil."

"Call Nancy and Isaac into worship," said her uncle sternly.

CHAPTER XXIII

A HAPPY EVENING AT EMERALD HILL

Domestic happiness thou only bliss
Of Paradise that has survived the fall!
—COWPER.

TWO evenings previous to the visitation Hugh and Oliver arrived at Emerald Hill on a Monday to Saturday Ministerial holiday; for in those days holidays except such were unknown to the clergy, who preached year in and year out as regularly as the sun rose and set. Another visitor had preceded them, a distant cousin of the minister's, who was governess in a Belfast family, and spent any few holidays she got at Emerald Hill where she was always made welcome.

Lucy Marshall was fat, fair and forty-five, cheerful and of placid temperament, and always grateful for any little pleasure that Fate grudgingly granted her, such as the present respite from six obstreperous children.

If only Mr. Shimmens would fancy Lucy! Hester often said to herself, she is so thankful for small mercies that it is possible she might even be grateful for him. Alas! Mr. Shimmens never deviated from the pursuit of his ideal.

The Emerald Hill parlour with its cheerful fire and well-spread table seemed to Oliver almost like Heaven, compared with his own lonely Manse and solitary uninviting meals, enlivened only by Ann's polite interrogations as to whether the potatoes were on "the hard side", or "the soft side", as the case might be; or whether "the green", a fearsome dish perpetrated by her, was "boiled to his taste".

The candles in their high brass candlesticks lighted up the friendly faces round, with that caressing touch that candlelight alone can give, while from behind the teacups there smiled on this lonely young hermit what he conceived to be the sweetest face in all the wide world.

The simple fare, blessed by the old minister, tasted good to palates unspoiled by luxuries. Nancy's hot potato cake swimming in butter was appreciated by the travellers. The Rev. Andrew himself liked a bit of oatcake, the good thick old-fashioned sort baked on the "griddle", and then placed around the turf ashes to dry thoroughly. A slice of toast made by the minister himself at the parlour fire was the basis of Mrs. Noble's meal. The boiled eggs tasted as those alone taste which have been eaten the same day as laid. Wheaten farls and soda farls enriched the table's variety, with dark luscious honey provided by the family bees, that held the distilled ambrosia of mountain heather and field flowers.

The discourse was of a serious pleasantness. Matters of Church and State were debated with knowledge and acumen. They spoke mostly of the Church's latest enterprise—the new theological college[14] shortly to be opened in Belfast by D'Aubigné the historian of the Reformation.

---

[14] **new theological college**: After mounting criticism of the training of Presbyterian ministers at the Academical Institution—"a seminary of Arianism" in Cooke's view—the Presbyterian College, known as 'Assembly's College' (today Union Theological College) was opened in 1853, with Cooke as its first President.

The Rev. Andrew Noble, whose whole heart, soul and being centred in the Church of his fathers, was filled with enthusiasm at this admirable step forward, and his face glowed in discussing it.

"The 'Institution' since its start," he said, "although built largely with the money of orthodox Presbyterians, has always been perniciously honeycombed by Arianism, and our students were in danger of imbibing that fearful heresy. Now that the Government has provided the Queen's Colleges for secular training, we have done the right thing in establishing a theological college staffed by those only who are sound in doctrine, so that our coming men may be firmly rooted and grounded in the Faith."

"Uncle," reminded his niece, "you're letting your tea get cold."

"And I consider it a beautiful structure," he resumed, after finishing his cup and handing it to her, "even in its architecture expressing outwardly the genius of Presbyterianism. Not ornate but solid and sturdy it stands to all the winds that blow."

Tea over, and the table pushed back against the wall to give room, the chairs were circled around the fire, and now that they were all near, Aunt Emily could join in the conversation.

The three ministers continued their discussions, while the three ladies talked of less learned matters. Mrs. Noble was anxious to hear from Lucy what was "the fashion" now in Belfast, and Hester naturally was interested in Lucy's description of bonnets and pelerines and other extinct articles then worn at that centre of fashion.

On this tranquil scene the door was suddenly

thrust open, and an unkempt head inserted.

"Well, how are yez enjoyin' yourselves?"

No one replied to the kind inquiry. Mrs. Noble looked witheringly at the intruder.

"Keep a good fire on to yourselves now. Will I bring you some more coal?"

"Please shut the door, Isaac," said his mistress with a shiver.

"Well, good night till yez all."

"Isaac," said the minister, "you will not go to bed until we have had worship. Call Nancy in."

Hester handed her uncle the large-typed Bible dedicated to this service. He moved to a chair beside his wife that she might clearly hear, and a hush fell on the little room.

"The second paraphrase:

> O God of Bethel by Whose Hand
> Thy people still are fed,
> Who through this weary pilgrimage
> Hast all our fathers led."

Hester's full young voice led them to the strains of St. Paul's. The majestic old tune rose and fell in solemn tones in the low-ceiled parlour. Mrs. Noble's weak voice was still true, but the old minister uttered strange sounds to those unaccustomed to them. Hugh and Oliver made more or less noise in their own way, Nancy sang harmoniously, but liked to drag behind in the old style. Lucy sang vigorously. All did their best in the matter of praise, except Isaac who remained soundless. He had stood up in "Meeting" mute all his life while the psalms were being sung, as so many Presbyterians do, who seem to get on their feet merely to show their tacit approval of what is going on. Never in Isaac's life had he attempted a note, and yet he could whistle delightfully. At the back of his mind lay the feeling that singing was altogether effeminate, and derogatory to the dignity of a robust ploughman.

The minister opened his Bible where the marker lay. Their portion that night was a full one. The magnificent pæan on Faith whose authorship is unknown, but which attests in its grandeur to the Sure Hand of God Himself. What wonders faith had wrought! They themselves were conscious of being in that noble succession. Oliver thought of his father battling his way through poverty and oppression by its leading; of his mother because of her sure vision seeing clearly in every trial beyond the veil. And what of himself? He also had already overcome obstacles. Once more he prayed that by its power he might ever be enabled to take a firm stand for God and the Right against the world.

They rose from their knees subdued by the hush that follows intercession. Nancy brought the bedroom candles. Peace descended on the little Christian household, and the Angel of the Lord had them in His Keeping.

CHAPTER XXIV

THE VISITATION OF PRESBYTERY

A dinner lubricates business.
— BOSWELL'S *Johnson*.

THE long anticipated "visitation" passed off satisfactorily to all parties concerned, as such formal functions seem to do.

The Rev. Andrew Noble preached a long doctrinal sermon while the Presbytery fidgeted more or less; for ministers above all others are seldom exemplary listeners to sermons. The singing was scarcely representative of the usual Taraghan praise service, in that it was reinforced by musicians from neighbouring congregations, but the Presbytery agreeably accepted it as a specimen, and it was specially commended in the "finding".

The elders answered a set series of questions regarding the minister's stewardship, commencing with the searching one—"Is your minister a man of piety?" Afterwards the minister was interrogated as to the proper performance of their vague duties.

While these matters of high import were being transacted in the Meeting-house, even more important affairs connected with the event were in progress in the Emerald Hill kitchen. To wit, the cooking of the visitation dinner.

Long before the "old hundredth" had been given out in the Meeting-house, a great roast had been placed on the "spit" before the turf fire, and here Nancy with two assistants, Mrs. McKibb, the wife of one of the elders, and a Miss Twigg, a notable housekeeper belonging to a neighbouring congregation, talked and perspired and got in each other's way, in the tremendous fuss necessary to the cooking of an ecclesiastical banquet, whilst scouts from the Meeting-house at intervals kept them informed of the stage of proceedings in "another place".

On each side of the red turf nestled "Dutch ovens" containing rice puddings generously pockmarked with large raisins, and others of bloated sago; both varieties luscious with eggs of the duck.

A red-headed youth thrust in his head at the door.

"The sarmon's over, an' they're startin' the questions," he reported.

This was Willie-John McKibb, the elder's son.

"Dear sen'," said Mrs. McKibb, "that your da will spake up, an' not be blate afore the Presbytery."

"Dear sen'," echoed Nancy, "that the pitaties will be done, an' them never on yet. Have you near finished with the peelin', Miss Twigg?"

"I'm just at the last one. Now, I'll give you a han' on with them. Lower the crook another hole. That's it. They'll not take long now. Well, that's so much forrad."

Nancy's anxiety took another turn.

"I hope to goodness the beef'll be done through. Wouldn't it be the quare spite to keep the Presbytery waitin' on their dinners, for some of them comes a long road an' must be feelin' the pits of their stomachs by now."

"Let it be soon or late," said Mrs. McKibb, ladling the dripping generously over the roast, "the

Presbytery never gets a dinner to bate Taraghan. Put on a lock more sods, Miss Twigg, to keep the beef sizzlin'."

"Aye, it would take us to keep up a brave fire," said Nancy, "for all must be ready on the bat of three."

"Don't fash yourself, Nancy," remonstrated Mrs. McKibb, "they'll just have to wait till it's ready; the Presbytery had to wait to be born."

"I wondher now," ruminated Nancy, "if it'll plaze the Reveren' Madill of Clegg. Miss McBlain, his housekeeper, tell me he's very notionate about his meat."

"Dear, but he's a bewitched lookin' craythur," remarked Miss Twigg, "you'd think to look at him he had been rared on crickets."

"Aye, an' shouldhers on him like a herrin'," supplemented Mrs. McKibb.

"Miss McBlain tells me," said Nancy, "that he wouldn't lip tay."

Derisive scorn greeted this announcement.

"It's well seen on him!" said Miss Twigg, shaking her head.

"It *is* that," agreed Mrs. McKibb. "Dear! what would we do on'y for the tay!"

"He's the quare odds now to the Reveren' McStay," commented Nancy, after lifting the lid of the potato pot and peering inside.

"Och, *he's* as fat as a killin' pig," said Mrs. McKibb. "Put on more turf on them oven lids, Miss Twigg, plaze, it takes a dale o' heat to swell that big sago out."

Miss Twigg did as she was directed, placing with

the tongs red lumps of peat on the oven lids. "Well," she said, when she had finished, "it's not on his steepins the Reveren' McStay thrives so well, for the Killykuffy people's very narra'."

"Thank goodness," ejaculated Nancy, "there's the white horses on the pitaties at last!"

"Shure everything's well forrad, Nancy, an' the Presbytery'll get it that it'll burn their mouths. Betther for them to have to spit it out, nor to have them give a shiver with every swally."

"I heerd tell," said Miss Twigg, "that at the ordination over beyant at Tullygig, they hadn't even a hot pitata—an' it a winther's day—cold beef, an' cold fowl an' cold ham with a bit of loaf bread along of it."

"Dear save us! it was enough to give the Presbytery a dwam in their insides," said Mrs. McKibb.

"They'll get no 'coul' kale' in Taraghan," boasted Nancy.

"Aye, but," whispered Miss Twigg, with a knowing shake of her head, "they had something to warm it when it went down."

"D'ye mind that now!" smiled Mrs. McKibb, leniently.

"Well, it would have been more fittin' for them *not*," asserted Nancy, "seein' their last man had to lave the counthry over the head of it. The masther an' two other ministers walked out from the table without bite or sup."

"Shure, they needn't have tasted it," objected Miss Twigg. "Couldn't they take it or leave it?"

"The masther said it was for a 'protest'."

"Oh, aye! you could count on our man doin' the

right thing," said Mrs. McKibb. "If there's a Christian man in the world this day it's our man!"

"I suppose your man's here the day, Miss Twigg, what soort of a visitor is he?" inquired Nancy.

"Well, he's nothin' to brag of. I was away from Meetin' three Sabbath days that time I had the touch o' brownkaties, afore he come to see about it, an' even then a neighbour man had to tell him. But by the time he come I was up an' met him at the door, an' I wasn't much more nor civil to him."

" 'It's newens to see you, Mr. Smillie,' sez I. Sez he, 'I'm very sorry to hear you were ill, but I only heard it last night.'

" 'I think I *was* ill,' sez I, 'an' the docter with me.'

"Sez he, in that quiet way he has of goin', 'How did the docter know you were ill?'

"Sez I, 'me brother had to go for him, for he couldn't get a wink with my cough at nights.' But he just smiled. No, there's no satisfaction in bein' angry with him."

"Well," said Nancy, "nobody can complain about the masther not visitin'. Isaac bees mad when he tells him to put the powny in the croydon till he pays some visits."

"Och, of coorse, he's one of the good oul' sort, but they're near han' all gone now. I seen the day when the coat was more respected nor the man is now inside it."

After this smashing verdict on the clergy, Mrs. McKibb took a potato from the pot and examined it critically. "They're on the hard side yet," she reported. "Any word of your man gettin' married yet, Miss Twigg?"

"Oh, aye! the people has him married time an' again, but he's single yet."

"I'm toul'," said Mrs. McKibb, "that's he's a great coortier."

"Well," said Miss Twigg, now up in arms for her own man, when others criticized him, "he's a tarrable well-set-up man, an' a good pullpit man forbye, an' my opinion is that he could get them he wanted."

"They say," said Nancy, placing various dishes on the table, and pouring boiling water over them to heat them, "they say he's lookin' money."

"Oh! shure they're all that," retorted Miss Twigg.

"I heerd," said Mrs. McKibb, "that he had a notion of thon rid-haired Miss Gabbey; she has lashin's of deeded property."

Miss Twigg snorted, "He wouldn't look at the side of the road she's on. I seen her at Killaghduffmoyle swarree, an' she's no beauty more nor myself, an' very nebbity lookin'."

"He's the quare good swarree speaker anyway," said Mrs. McKibb, "I heerd him that night meself, an' you could have tied me with a straw."

"Here's Willie-John runnin'," said Nancy, looking through the window, "it must be near over—Well, Willie-John?"

"They're just beginnin' the last paraphrase."

"Well, run you over, Willie-John, to Mrs. Macrory's an' see if the chickens is ready."

"I'm just afther bein' there, she says they're done to pieces."

"That's right! Gimme a han' with the pot, Miss Twigg, till I teem the pitaties."

"Show me the beetle, Nancy, an' I'll champ them. I mustn't be like the servant-girl when the masther got a lump in the champ an' asked her the meanin' of it. 'Oh! that one just escaped the beetle, sir,' sez she."

"Now, all's ready," said Nancy. "Here's the dish for the beef, Mrs. McKibb. Put the dish cover on it, Miss Twigg. Wait till I give it a wee rub. Now, that's Protestant lookin'. Willie-John, away with you with it an' lay it down afore the schoolhouse fire, an' don't be there till you're back again for the gravy. The ministhers all likes their fill of gravy. Miss Twigg, will you folly him with the pitaties an' see that everythin's set right on the table. Miss Hester will give it the finishin' touches when she goes in. Will you take the puddens on the tray, Mrs. McKibb? An' I'll stay here to give them more hot pitaties when they want them."

Nancy sat down by the open door and wiped the perspiration from face and neck, conscious that she had performed no mean part in the success of the day. Perhaps, indeed, it may have been largely due to her share of the proceedings that the Presbytery, after doing "ample justice" to the abundant fare provided, formulated a "finding" congratulating Taraghan on minister, elders, and church property, adding a polite recommendation at the end, to a little more generosity to the various funds of the church—a harmless exhortation—for nobody gave a halfpenny more on account of it.

They appointed the Rev. Mr. Smillie, of Killaghduffmoyle, to preach in Taraghan, and read the "finding" to the people.

CHAPTER XXV

WATCHING AND PRAYING

To see her is to love her and love but her for ever.
— BURNS.

WORSHIP in the mornings was always held in Mrs. Noble's bedroom. Previously to this Isaac had cleaned the grate and lighted the fire. He was particularly successful in evoking the fire spirit, and believed himself the only one in the house capable of it. Leaving dancing flames behind, he would retire amid much clatter and protest, remarking to the bed, "Dear, but you're happy lyin' there this coul' weather." He himself had never lain in bed one day in his life.

When prayers were about to commence, however, rarely could Isaac be found, or if ambushed, he was outraged at the suggestion that he should quit the important business he had in hand, insinuating that such dereliction would bring the whole place to rack and ruin. His master would sigh deeply over this deplorable attitude of his servant-man and in a chastened tone give out the psalm or paraphrase.

Mrs. Noble's bedroom was low-ceiled, and the red roses that had bloomed on its carpet at one stage of its existence had, like herself, faded and got wan, but the room possessed a glory that loftier and more ornate chambers might well envy. Its wide old-fashioned window revealed a prospect such as could not be viewed without drawing the heart nearer the Infinite. Before it towered the peaks of the

Mourne Mountains in their ever-changing awesome grandeur, while in the near foreground spread the woods that surrounded Castle Dingle.

Mrs. Noble might be exonerated if lying in her four-poster, gazing on that sublime panorama, she should cling to her bed perhaps more than was necessary.

Nancy removed the tray, smoothed the coverlet, and made to disappear certain of the minister's habiliments, for, on the matter of tidiness, his womankind found fault alone with him. The place now being considered presentable, she informed the breakfast table that "the mistress was ready for worhsip any time".

This morning there was quite a small congregation, and chairs had to be fetched from the other bedrooms. Nancy, who knelt between the window and the door, fidgeted somewhat, and even at times envied Isaac's godless tactics, as she sniffed to catch any smell of burning from saucepans that perchance she had forgotten on the fire. Then conscience-stricken she would close her eyes tight and do her best to follow her master's world-wide petitions.

On this morning she happened to open her eyes and glance out of the window, and failed to close them again, so transfixed were they on something outside the spiritual world. Scarcely could she keep on her knees till the long-deferred "Amen" came, and even after that it tried her patience to await the uprising of the minister, who from a sense of fitness and also an increasing stiffness, was always the last to get on his feet.

"Look! look!" she shouted, pointing at the

window, "thonder's a bird like the one in the mistress's sampler down in the parlour. It must be a phaysan'."

It was indeed a magnificent pheasant in fine plumage carrying its long wedge-shaped tail with dignity as it strutted on the lawn before them, seemingly conscious of admiration.

As they stood around the window following its graceful movements, and commenting on its beauty, suddenly there rang out a shot and the gay trespasser tumbled over and lay still. It was only then they noticed the absence of the minister.

"Dear, but the masther's the gran' shot," admired Nancy.

Mrs. Temple wished very much to know what they were looking at, and was informed of the handsome bird and its fate.

"I thought I heard a shot," she said, "who could have done such a thing? Was it Isaac?"

"Mebbe so," said Nancy, with the least smile at the others.

"I am exceedingly angry with him. Please tell him so," said his mistress.

At this juncture the minister entered, quarry in hand.

"It was most wicked of Isaac to shoot Lord Dingle's pheasant, and dreadfully cruel too," said Mrs. Noble.

The minister had no intention of anyone else getting either the credit or blame.

"I shot the bird," he declared.

"You!"

"I, myself."

"Oh! Andrew, how could you be so cruel?"

"It would have been shot anyway one of these days, and I did it cleanly."

"But the pheasant wasn't yours."

"Wasn't it?"

"No, it was Lord Dingle's."

"Heaven directed it to me and I received it. Wasn't I right, Oliver?"

"Nothing wrong in spoiling the Egyptians," assented Oliver stoutly.

"Lady Dingle is most kind to me," protested Mrs. Noble.

"Yes, she patronizes you, and sends you jellies by her footman, but her forefathers robbed mine. Their day will come, too."

"We must hasten it," said Oliver.

"You'll likely live to see it, but I shall be where landlords are not. Couldn't we have it for dinner, Hester?"

"Oh, no, not to-day, uncle, it must 'hang'."

"We must have it before our visitors leave."

"You want us all to share in your crime, father," said Hugh.

"And I shall sport the feathers," said Hester.

"I shall have nothing to say to it," declared Mrs. Noble.

"There'll be the more for the rest of us, Mamma," said her son.

....

As the two servants sat at dinner in the kitchen, Nancy dramatically related to Isaac the stupendous event of the morning.

"Sez the mistress, sez she, 'Tell Isaac I am very angry with him,' and with that in comes the masther houlin' up the phaysan', an' she pulls the clothes over her head."

"Why, but you let her think it was me, and I would have got the good scouldin'? I'm more used to it nor the masther."

" 'I myself done it,' sez he, in his gran' pullpit way."

Isaac shook his head. "Every word's an oath with him," he said. "Do you mind the sellin' of thon big gazaybo of a kickin' horse? Sez the masther to me when I was gettin' him ready for the fair, 'Isaac, I rely on you to inform the buyer that he has a facetious habit of kickin'.' 'All right,' sez I, 'lave that all to me.' 'Isaac,' sez he, 'I *command* you not to sell this animal under false pretences.' But when me oul'farned boy of a hoss was put through his paces, nivver a kick did he give an' thinks I to myself mebbe he has got convarted, an' why would I blacken his kerechter. So I sowl him to a man that wanted a big strong baste for cartin'.

"A wheen o' days afther, didn't I see the man comin' up to the front dure as His Reverence was just goin' out; so I hid in the scrubbery an' heerd the whole piece.

"Sez the man, 'Are you the Rev. Andrew Noble?'

" 'I am that same,' sez the masther.

" 'Your sarvint sowl' me a hoss in Ballydiggelty Fair,' sez the man.

" 'I hope you have not suffered from his misfortunate habit of kicking,' sez the masther.

" 'That's just my errand here,' sez the man, 'for

I come all the way to tell you, that I just hadn't the time on me han's to make a new cart *ivery* mornin'.'

"I could have split me sides at that, for many's the mornin' I had to start with nailin' boards!

" 'I wouldn't have give what I did if I had knowed that he had that fault,' sez the man. An' if the masther didn't away till his desk an' give him what he asked for! Dear, but it would be the joke of the world to see His Reverence in the fair sellin' a horse! It would do for the newspapers!"

"Aw well! If anybody gets to heaven it'll be the masther," said Nancy.

"They don't sell horses in heaven," said Isaac.

....

Oliver and Hester paced the garden paths that golden afternoon, their bodies warmed by the autumn sun that always seems so much more loving than that of summer, like an old friend who grows tenderer as the time of his departure draws near. Their hearts also glowed in unison warmed by the close companionship. Close at Hester's heels paced old Roger, a dog of mixed pedigree, who had long suspected their visitor of designs on his young mistress, and felt it his duty to protect her.

For the most part Hester talked and her lover listened. Then there fell sweet silences in which their spirits seemed to mingle. And all the while the withered leaves dropped at their feet, warning them that we pay forfeit for happiness; that sooner or later in our lives come the falling leaves.

How he longed to tell her of his love! But what had he to offer? How could he propose to take her from this comfortable home and bring her into one of poverty and anxiety? His stipend and *regium donum*[15] together did not amount to a great deal over a hundred pounds. His Manse was as yet meagrely furnished. He must wait.

And meanwhile she would certainly be sought after; for Oliver believed that no man could look on her and not desire her. Even Mr. Shimmens he still feared, with his prosperous congregation, and means necessarily accumulated by years of bachelorhood. His faithful heart was a medley of hopes and fears that conspired to keep his tongue silent.

Lower and lower sank the sun. Already the glory was departing as they turned indoors. Tea-time came and the cheerful fire, and after that the three ministers read; at least Oliver held a book in his hand, as he sat beside Hester, apparently hypnotized by the gaily-coloured wools of her embroidery. She was working a picture in "Berlin" work of a delightfully impudent-looking King Charles spaniel, enthroned on a gorgeous crimson cushion, from each corner of which was suspended a silken tassel. Her round flushed cheek bent over the work and her hands caressed its growing beauty. Lucy was engrossed in her "white work", and Mrs. Noble held in her hand a book—the life of some sainted minister—and frankly dozed. Taking advantage of a slight altercation between Hugh and his father on some point of orthodoxy, Oliver whispered into the ear next him, "I wish I was that little dog!"

---

[15] **regium donum**: a government grant to the Presbyterian clergy in Ireland. It was discontinued in 1869.

CHAPTER XXVI

THE WEDDING OF ADAM AND MARTHA

The end crowns all.

—SHAKESPEARE.

ADAM CLEMENTS'S courtship continued according to his own deliberate methods, until Mrs. Tuffit, Mrs. McIlroy and even Mr. Moynagh were anxious and willing to bring matters to a crisis.

On Monday mornings (Adam never having failed to escort Martha home on Sabbath night) William Moynagh would say in his loud hearty way:

"Any word of the weddin', Adam?"

"What weddin'?"

"Your own, man dear! Shure you're walkin' Matty McIlroy years. Now, I was only courtin' six weeks myself."

"Man oh! but you done it suddint."

"Well, they say marriage comes like a soot drop, but I'm afraid the whole chimney'll fall before you get the lines."

"Wouldn't it be tarrible if a body rued it when it was done?"

"I never rued it for one mortyal minute."

"Aye, but you got the misthress."

"I did *that*! I must have had some poor body's blessin'."

"It's a sayrious jab."

Mr. Moynagh's face was anything but "sayrious". "I heard," said he, "that one night you kissed her goin' up the loanen."

"The fool! did she tell it?"

His master's laugh reached Mrs. Moynagh in the parlour behind, and Adam wondered what on earth the joke was.

Mrs. McIlroy was wont to attack her daughter thus:

"You'll have the quare aisy life of it forbye marryin' a farmer. Look at the lady you'll be! sellin' poun's of tea and sugar over your own counter. There's a quare odds in that, an' ploughin' through a yard of clabber to feed pigs. Now, Adam's a studdy boy, an' could set up for himself if he wanted. I wouldn't put it past him to have fifty poun' in the bank!"

Martha would pretend to disinclination in the matter.

"Och! Ma, let me be; he's oul', he's forty if he's a day."

"He'll be fifty if you don't give him a dunch; he's blate, that's what he is."

And Mrs. Tuffit argued thus:

"It'll be the quare day for you when you get a good Presbyterian. Your poor da was a Methody, but he knows betther now, whoever's talkin' till him. If you get married in meetin', I'll give the weddin', an' I'll do it clever, an' you an' Adam can sit in the sate with me afther it. Has he bespoke you yet?"

"I b'lieve he'll never get it out."

"I'll spake to him," offered Mrs. Tuffit grandly.

"You will not, aunt, for I'm in swithers whether I'll take him or not. I'd thank yez all not to interfere, but let things take their coorse."

Nevertheless, the very next Sabbath evening as Adam and she neared the loanen that led to her home, Martha broke the silence.

"Do you know what the people's sayin'?" she asked.

"No, what?" said Adam somewhat startled.

"That you an' me's goin' to get married agin harvest!"

"Well! well! Now, I wondher who started that clash. Won't they get the quare gunk?"

"Mebbe not," maintained Martha.

Adam turned and looked at her in some astonishment.

"Were you thinkin' of gettin' married?" he queried.

"What do you think I was keepin' company with you for?"

"Oh, aye, in the end we might. Do you think we wouldn't rue it?"

"Everybody has to chance that," said the philosophic Martha.

There was silence for the space of five minutes while Adam's brain struggled with the situation. "Where would we live if we got married?"

"Here, of coorse," said Martha, "there's only me ma an' William James, an' it would be convenyent to Innis for you."

The most formidable lion, however, remained yet to be cleared out of Adam's path.

"You'd have to get married in the Meetin'-house, if ever it comes to that."

"That's what I'm goin' to do. Aunt Tuffit an' me has it all laid out. We're to sit in her sate on Sundays afther it."

The precipitancy of womankind left poor Adam dumbfounded.

"Well! well!" he said, grasping at last the fact that he was betrothed, "it's well me father and mother are both in their graves afore I married a Methodist. They would have been neither to hold nor to bind."

"Shure I was only half a one. Just wait till you see the good Presbytern I'll make. Turncoats always do that."

. . . .

The engagement was announced immediately, and preparations forthwith set in train for the festival. It was generally conceded that Martha was making a brilliant match from the social aspect, and as for other points of view, Adam was proclaimed by the elders to be the making of a model husband. It was arranged that the wedding would take place before the good weather went, and on a late sunny autumn day Martha McIlroy was at long last transformed into Mrs. Adam Clements.

Mrs. Tuffit was determined that it would be the event of the season—indeed, of many seasons for that matter—and invitations to far and near relatives and friends were issued, all of which were promptly accepted. The house could in no way contain the bidden guests, but Mrs. Tuffit was a woman of resource. She had the barn cleared out, whitewashed and scrubbed. She borrowed kitchen tables which placed end to end resulted in one magnificent banqueting board, and she had forms fetched from the schoolhouse to seat the revellers.

Not since the Revival meetings had Ballydaisy Meeting-house enclosed so many human beings, so that it was with difficulty that the bride's party pushed their way up the aisle to where Adam awaited. The bride and bridesmaid—a "comrade girl" of Martha's called Agnes Meharg—wore dresses of blue silk over crinolines, and except that that of the bride had a veil, similar white poke bonnets. The traditional pallor was absent from Martha's face, which resembled a full-blown peony rose. Mrs. Tuffit and Mrs. McIlroy wore Paisley shawls new for the occasion over black silk dresses.

Adam was sitting in the front seat on their arrival, and continued to sit until William James McIlroy told him in a stage whisper to "stan' on his feet".

This being accomplished the simple service commenced.

There was a slight pause when the bridegroom was asked if he were willing to take the person whom he held by the right hand to be his lawful wedded wife, but in the end he admitted he was. Martha's avowal was low and positive. After which Oliver pronounced them man and wife, and prayed for a blessing on the union.

Such a string of jaunting cars as left the Meeting-house gate had never been witnessed before. Each with its full complement of two, or even in some cases three aside, and perhaps an extra in "the well". In this wise started the triumphal procession for Mrs. Tuffit's.

Along the route people leant over half-doors cheering. Those who lived up "loanens" took up positions on the high road and joined with gusto in the acclamation. All onlookers declared it was a grand "turn-out", and such as could not be surpassed for splendour.

"Dear, but the blue becomes her!"

"Aye, doesn't she set it quare an' well, for her cheeks is redder nor apples."

"An' he looks smartened up too in that grey shute with the gereenium in his buttonhole."

"If he would only look as if he wasn't goin' till his own funeril."

"She's gettin' a good boy anyway, he nayther drinks nor smokes, an' as regular at Meetin' as the ministher."

"She's a brave wee girl herself. Do you think will she come till Ballydaisy Meetin' with him, or take him with her?"

"No fear! Adam's the rale oul' blackmouth."

"Well, if he brings her till Meetin' it'll be a good jab."

"It will that!"

"Look, if thon's not her cousin Sammy Lilley from Belfast on the next car! I would know his skin on a thorn bush."

"That's the very boy, an' him with the airs an' appearance of a gentleman."

"They tell me he's an eldher now in some Belfast Meetin'."

"Boys-a-boys! I mind him the riotest wee rascal roun' Ballydaisy."

"Aye, wasn't he a tarror? But d'ye mind him gettin' the prize for sayin' the Catechism off? An' sez the ministher that examined him (he was a furriner to these parts from up about Portydown), sez he, 'my boy you are a credit to the neighbourhood.' I think I sees him pattin' Sammy on the head, an' me brave boy lookin' as if butther wouldn't melt in his mouth. An' that very same evenin', afore he went till his bed, an' him afther repeatin' the whole of the Shorter Catechism off without one mistake, didn't he kill Mrs. McWha's darlin' young drake with a stone!"

"Thon would be his mistress sittin' alongside of him. Did you ever set eyes on such gran'yeur?"

"Her clothes is very gran', but he must have picked her in the dark. She's tarrible blackavised, an' looks to me to have a wee bit of skelly."

"She'll not tear in the pluckin' anyway."

"They say her father's as rich as a Jew an' has pawnshops in Belfast."

"I wouldn't put it past her to be a Jew herself. Them black eyes isn't very Protestant lookin'."

"Here's Mr. and Mrs. Moynagh next. Isn't she the darlin' of a woman, not a bit of politeness about her, an' her could have anything she likes."

"Aye, he would give her anything. I never seen a man thought such a dale of a woman."

"An' if there's not oul' Andy McFerran, the widda man, him that's on the lookout for a third! Look at the cut of him, will you, with his dyed side-whiskers an' his check shute!"

"I heerd tell that he dyes them wi' ink, an' that one tarrible wet Sunday he come into Ballydaisy Church with black lines all over his face like a gridiron. It's well he got a sate on a car for he's just hirplin' along."

"Aye, an' it nearly bates him to sit on it, for that hoss is very ree, an' Andy has to houl' on by the dickey."

"Some people's plazed to say he has a notion of Mrs. Tuffit herself."

"Aye, she's the pickle next the wind, an' it would be the gran' sittin'down for him, but I hear she gives out she'll never take another."

"She'll not take *him* anyway, for he's an Episcopal an' she's a true-blue."

"There she is herself on the last car, isn't she the sonsy big woman? Look at the way she weighs her side down, you'd think it would cowp."

"Aye, she's like the side wall of a house."

And to similar remarks of admiration or disparagement the calvacade swept on. The critics invariably remarking that "long sickness was death at last", before returning to their ordinary avocations stimulated by the entertainment.

Arrived at Mrs. Tuffit's door Adam with sudden inspiration gallantly lifted his bride off the car, and set her on her feet.

The guests poured in. Soon the parlour overflowed into the kitchen, where as Andy McFerran declared the very smell would do your inside good, such was the aroma arising from spits, pots, pans and Dutch ovens.

The wedding feast was ready, neighbours having undertaken the cooking during the ceremony. There ensued a delightful bustle of "dishing-up" by the ladies, whilst the gentlemen of the party bore the viands to the glorified barn.

On an immense platter lay an enormous quarter of what had once been a placid cow.

"Gimme the beef ma'am," proffered he of the dyed whiskers and check suit, anxious to win Mrs. Tuffit's regard by his eager service.

"It'll take an able-bodied man for that," said she

cruelly, "*you* might lave it in smithereens on the street.

"Hi! William John, will you hoist the beef to the barn? Here Mr. McFerran take you the kebbige an' watch your feet goin' up the barn steps."

When all the dishes had disappeared Mrs. Tuffit followed and arranged them. The beef took precedence at the head of the table, while a roast of mutton held a minor honour at the foot. Interspersed between lay hens and chicks and hams, relieved by mountains of potatoes.

The hostess returning to the house, marshalled her company and sent them forth two by two, arm in arm to the banquet. The minister and herself brought up the rear.

Quiet reigned till after the "blessing". Afterwards a babel of voices grew and increased. All were out to enjoy themselves and proclaimed the fact. It was a day that rarely came in their calendar, and as they would have said, "a day by itself."

Soon it was necessary to shout if addressing a friend across the table. Guest encouraged guest, nay, challenged him to gastronomic feats.

"Come an' we'll make a bate which of us'll ate the most," said William James McIlroy, the best man, to Thomas McKeever, a tall narrow-chested bachelor of sallow complexion.

"I dursn't," said Tammas sadly, "for I'm of a beelious disposition."

"Why, man, the cure for that's constant atin'. Here aunt, give him another wee whack of beef." Thomas's plate was forcibly removed, and after journeying up the table returned to him with something of everything it had passed on the way like islands surrounded by an ocean of gravy. "Now, fall-to man an' don't say when you go home that you didn't get enough."

"Andy! hoy Andy!" was heard above the clamour, "they say yours'll be the next big day."

"What's that you're sayin'?" said Andy, putting his hand behind his ear.

"That you an' thon Miss Timp's castin' sheeps' eyes at other across Ballydaisy Church."

"Well," said Andy, "it would need to be done wi' the eyes, for she's that deef that if you wanted to tell her anything private you'd have to take her into the middle of a field. But I'm waitin' on Tammas McKeever here to go first. They say he's puttin' spake on a widda woman."

"But she's still in weeds for her man."

"To be sure! the veil's a good signboard!"

"Here's Geordie Welsh on the lookout too," said someone.

A freckled youth flushed painfully, and fixed his attention on the mutton on his plate.

"Don't heed them, son," said William Moynagh, "though that would be natural enough for Geordie, but an old fool's the worst of a fool."

There were also some respectful jokes at the minister's lonely condition.

"An' mind, Mr. Whiteside, what you're doin' an' don't get a wife like the Reverend Sankey's of Trelogue, I declare that woman does everything barrin' gettin' intil the pullpit."

"More's the pity she doesn't do that too," said the bridesmaid, "for thon oul' sing-song voice of his would put you over afore he finishes givin' out the text."

"But that's betther nor to split your head like the Rev. Smithers of Tumulty. They do say that the people near the pullpit bees deef on Mondays. The wondher is that the roof stays on Tumulty Meetin'-house!"

"Now," reproved the hostess, "you're all talkin' in place of eatin', pass your plates for a piece of fowl an' ham, for the beef's only first coorse."

"It's the gran' beef, so it is," said Andy McFerran, "an' I didn't enjoy a meal as much since Elias Twigg's funeril."

"If yous think the meat's good show it," said Mrs. Tuffit. "All of yez make yourselves at home, though I don't wish you there. Will ye accept a wee leg of fowl, Mr. Wilkison?"

"No, I thank you, ma'am, I'm as full as a tick." Notwithstanding this unblushing declaration, Mr. Wilkinson's plate was whipped from under his nose, and came back with the leg of a rooster extending beyond its borders.

A scrum followed. Plates were seized while their possessors were caught unawares. It often took the strength of both hands to retain one in its owner's possession.

"Why Tammas, you done nothin' at all," said his hostess reproachfully.

"I'm just afeard I ate too hearty," said Thomas, "I'm full up to the throat."

"You'll have to make room for the puddens," said William James.

"We're not near ready for them yet," said the

hostess. "Would you take a wee bit more of the breast, Mrs. Lilley?"

"I have quite sufficient, thank you," said the Belfast lady. Never, thought her suburban ladyship, had she witnessed such a vulgar scene.

Knives and forks clattered on plates, sighs were heaved, and buttons loosed, but Mrs. Tuffit was quite plaintive. "It was hardly worth your whiles sittin' down," she said, and resigned herself to the removal of what remained of the beef with its satellites, and the substituting of great sago and rice puddings of a glowing saffron, flanked by jugs of cream.

Heaped plates once more passed round, and some valiant trenchermen actually cleared them, but, for the most part, larger or smaller mounds were left.

Lastly arrived a tray of glasses, Mrs. Tuffit remarking: "Just a wee dhrap to keep yez all from the indisgestion."

Oliver could have borne his testimony better before a hostile crowd. The real kindness, the good fellowship around him made it immeasurably more difficult. It was no easy matter for him to say: "You will please excuse me, Mrs. Tuffit, and I'll take a turn in the garden."

"Mr. Whiteside! Surely, you'll take a wee glass."

"No thank you, I am pledged against it for ever."

As he strolled down the loanen he felt he had hurt the feelings of his hostess, and earned the disapproval of his fellow-guests.

Someone touched him on the arm. It was the cousin from Belfast.

"I'm with you, Mr. Whiteside," he said, "the Rev. William Johnston asked all of us elders to sign the pledge."

"That is the good of signing," said Oliver, "for no decent person would insist on you breaking it. It is better than argument."

Ah! those Temperance Pioneers! It is impossible now to comprehend their bravery. Derided, and in cases persecuted, they endured all things, hoped all things, believed all things. They were men "sent to the Kingdom for such a time". A new revelation has been vouchsafed them and they did not hesitate to obey its commands, cost them what it would. "There were giants in those days!"

....

The male revellers streamed out to cool themselves in the crisp October air, while the womankind helped with the washing up of the dishes.

Two hours afterwards, however, found the barn inhabited again. Now the table groaned under thickly sliced currant cakes, and carraway cakes, and butter and cheese and jam and honey. Mrs. Tuffit at one end and Mrs. McIlroy at the other poured out strong cups of tea heavily sugared. When all were served one cup still remained. They were one short, and an alarm was raised.

It proved to be Thomas McKeever.

"He must be out-bye," said Mrs. Tuffit.

"I'll go and saarch for him," offered William James McIlroy, leaving the table.

No trace of the absentee could he find. "Mebbe he's takin' a look at the kettle," he said to himself, thrusting his head into the byre.

And there was Thomas lying on some hay in the corner!

"Why, Tammas, man, what's wrong wi' ye?"

"I'm dyin' wi' beeliousness. I'm dyin' this time."

"Nobody ever died of that, come on in an' take your tay, there's lashins of currant bread."

"Lave me me lone, it would kill me out to set eyes on it! I can't lift me head. Lave me me lone."

Which William James did, and returned and informed the company that "Tammas was lyin' in the byre, near his latther end wi' beeliousness."

It is heartless to record that instead of casting a gloom over the guests, this announcement caused their merriment so to overflow that the sound thereof reached the defeated victim in his lowly lair. Although their spirits seemed capital previously, now they were hilarious.

Each vied with his neighbour in telling comical stories chiefly bearing on the risks of matrimony.

"D'ye mind oul' Paddy and Biddy Molloy? Biddy was the priests's housekeeper an' a heartscald to him, an' he palmed her off on poor Paddy who was lookin' a wife. A week afterwards he called to see how they were doin' an' met Paddy down the loanen. Sez he, 'Well, Paddy, how are you an' Biddy getting along?'

"An' with that Paddy raises his hands, 'Yer Reverence thon woman you married me on is worse nor the divil.'

" 'For shame, Paddy!' sez the priest, 'such a thing could not be.'

" 'Well,' sez Paddy, 'I can prove it to you out of the Scriptures, for they say that if you resist the divil he'll fly from you, but if you resist *her* she'll fly *at* you.' "

Laughter and applause.

"D'ye mind Margit Smart?" said another.

"Orange Margit?"

"Aye, that was her nickname. She used to cry when she heerd tell of anybody gettin' married, an' said she'd rather hear tell of their funeril any day."

"Robert had a tarrable life wi' her, she was that thriftless."

"Aye, an' took a dhrap a long while before the people foun' out."

"She would put her han' over her mouth an' say, 'Dear, don't come near me, I was atin' onions.' "

"She was a great Protestan'."

"She was that. If you were talkin' till her out in a field with nobody in sight, she would be lookin' all roun' her an' whisper, 'but you couldn't say a word for them Papishes listenin'.' "

"When Robert would scold, she would take down the Bible an' read it out as loud as she could to dhrown him."

"He was a big gomish of a man not to lave her. What that man stood the divil wouldn't stan'."

These reminiscences, which were more or less of this marital flavour, were not one would have thought exactly reassuring to the pair who had that very day launched their barque on the avowedly perilous voyage. Nevertheless, until the end of time, those just embarking will hold fast the claim that their course will be calmer and fairer and brighter than any that have preceded it. Nature sees to this illusion.

After tea, the bride and bridegroom set out on their car for home. The entire company (minus

Thomas) escorted it as it bumped down the loanen and emerged on the county road.

The driver whipped up his horse. The ladies waved their handkerchiefs, and the men their hats, and all cheered till the happy pair had turned the corner out of sight. Only then did someone remember the hapless "Tammas", and all went in a body to visit him.

"Get up man dear, an' me an' Willie Wilkison'll oxthercog you till Mrs. Moynagh's car. They're goin' to convoy you home."

This was accomplished successfully, and "Tammas" was conveyed there lying across "the well".

All now prepared to depart. Mrs. Tuffit was overwhelmed with congratulations on the splendour and lavishness of the entertainment, and all professed that never in their lives had they eaten so much before.

"An' as for the divarshun," said Willie Wilkinson, "the sight of Tammas lyin' in the byre bate all the sets I ever seen. Never again will I be able to look at him liftin' the ha-pence in Ballydaisy Meetin' an' keep my face straight. Isn't it a marcy he didn't take to the pig-crue!"

A tired woman was Mrs. Tuffit that night. But her exaltation of mind completely compensated for that trifling sensation. As she laid her head on the pillow she said to herself: "I done my duty anyway, with the help of Goodness and my own smartness, I saved her from bein' a Methody, an' got her a true-blue Presbyterian. Thank the Lord for all his mercies!"

CHAPTER XXVII

NEWCASTLE

> It is a goodly sight to see
> What Heaven hath done for this delicious land.
> — BYRON.

DEAR to the hearts of loyal County Down natives is that gem of nature known as Newcastle, or, as the country folk call it "Newkessel", nestling'neath Slieve Donard Mountain, the "Monarch of Mourne". A Beulah-land "whose air is very sweet and pleasant and that borders on Heaven".

Newcastle has played a prominent part in their well-ordered lives and those of their fathers before them. One generation passes away after another, who have counted a sojourn by its sounding sea above their chief joy, as well as a certain antidote to all the ills that bodily flesh is heir to during the long Northern winter.

At the time of our story "Newkessel" was idyllic in its primitive simplicity. Demure little cottages sitting in patches of gay old-fashioned flowers serenely contemplated the ebb and flow of the tide. On and on "Newkessel" straggled of its own sweet will and even attempted to climb the mountain-side.

Never as long as Andrew Noble could remember had he missed a summer stay at Newcastle. The family jaunting car of his youth covered the distance of seventeen miles in half a day. The farm cart likewise made its journey carrying provisions; potatoes, oatmeal, home-cured ham and bacon, home-made cheese, butter, and eggs.

The family relieved each other at home, so that all might benefit by a fortnight's ozone, such as they fully believed could not be obtained in any other quarter of the globe.

Even when Providence assigned to the young minister a future residence much nearer this delectable spot, the annual visit thither continued to be an unbroken rule of his artless life. While staying there, he drove, or sometimes indeed walked, to conduct the services in his own congregation. Holidays from preaching were in those days undreamt of: nay, ministers cherished opportunities for showing forth the way of salvation. The difficulty rather was in the Rev. Andrew Noble's case, to restrain him from preaching on week-days, and at all times and seasons, in his own house or that of anyone else.

The transit of Mrs. Noble was a matter of concern comprising as it did much invalid equipment, and various books of devotion. Her entourage also included two hens. They gained a seaside holiday on certain conditions—namely, that each contribute an egg *per diem* to their mistress's bill of fare. Now, Mrs. Noble could detect unerringly the age of an egg, and a twenty-four hours' old specimen she rejected as "not quite fresh". Thus, while the household consumed cheerfully the weekly supply brought by Isaac from Emerald Hill, together with butter, vegetables, etc., she had at command a steady source of authentic sustenance. Should, however, one of these feathered favourites forget her duty in the allurements of picking up dainties by the seaside, she was ignominiously dispatched home, and replaced by another red-head cackling candidate, appointed to take up the duties of this responsible position.

The family were now approaching the last week of their stay, a period eagerly looked forward to by Hester from the very beginning. For Hugh had invited Oliver to share then his narrow bed, and inhale a week's tonic air.

The day dawned at length, as all days longed for or dreaded have hitherto since the creation of the world. It was a morning after rain when the very air that touched the cheek smelt sweet, and the bluish-green waves stole in nearer and nearer.

On the garden seat in front of his cottage sat, or rather was enthroned, the Rev. Andrew Noble, happier than any king. His spirit reacted to a sense of God's goodness over all His works, and this sensibility flooded his receptive soul with an ineffable peace, that was in harmony with the surpassing beauty of his immediate surroundings. A villa on the Riviera would not have compensated the County Down minister for that small whitewashed cottage on the Newcastle shore.

He sat awaiting the fishman, but he was not permitted to make the purchase. That was one thing above all others of which he was considered grossly incapable.

As he sat at peace with all the world, he watched with kindly interest the folk passing in ones and twos and threes, in that purposeless progression peculiar to the seaside. Most of the male portion doffed their hats to him, while the womenkind smiled pleasantly. For was he not a "Newkessel" institution, and an inseparable item of their holiday experience? He raised his hat and gave all, unknown, or partly known, or only guessed at, a look of goodwill and blessing.

Before the arrival of the fishman the seat had, as was usually the case, overflowed, mostly with elders, or his brethren in the Ministry, and he was obliged to bring out a chair for himself. But he who kept it warmest was the Rev. Obadiah Shimmens, whose Newcastle holiday invariably coincided with that of Emerald Hill.

The conversation on these occasions was markedly "Presbyterial". On listening one would never infer that either communions also existed in Ulster, so oblivious of such were the discourses. Not the College of Cardinals itself could discuss with more composed pretension the procedures and deliberations and decrees of "The Church". The Ulster Presbyterian is born with the confidence that to be a Presbyterian is what the Almighty intended a man to be, and if he ever forsakes the Church of his fathers for pulpit or pew of another, there is one thing sure, that it is not from conviction! It is this world—not the other—he is out to gain!

These congenial friends had gone; all excepting Mr. Shimmens who could out-sit the tardiest, by the time the fishcart drawn by a donkey hove in sight. Women appeared at various doors plate in hand, and after a little perhaps heated exchange retreated with more or less heaped dishes. The donkey had now arrived almost opposite Pansy Cottage, whereupon its deputed occupant moved to the open door, and in a voice that never failed to reach the farthest pew, shouted "Nancy!" From somewhere far within a shriller voice responded: "Houl' him till I come."

This the minister did, metaphorically, in pleasant conversation regarding the weather, and suitable allusions to "the harvest of the sea", until Nancy hurrying out with a dish and without any polite preliminaries, inquired the price.

"How many do you stan' in need of?" parried the fishman.

"Mebbe half a dozen of the wee flat ones."

"That'll be sixpence," said the fishman calmly.

"And little enough," interposed the minister, "considering the peril undergone to acquire them."

"Away an' talk to Mr. Shimmens, don't lave him all his lone," urged Nancy. Then archly to the fishman, as though his remark was intended to be humorous, "four-pence you mean."

The fishman was deeply offended. "They cost me more than that meself," he said, "but just on account of His Reverence I'll make it fippence."

At this crisis, a very tall and very dignified clergyman with a graceful gliding carriage approached the little green gate, the sight of whom caused the Rev. Andrew to spring to his feet, and seize the stranger's hand eagerly.

"Why, Professor! come in, come in, I was afraid you had gone and I had missed seeing you." And he led him joyfully to the garden seat, where also the visitor was greeted by Mr. Shimmens with deferential courtesy.

The fishman, who had drawn aside respectfully, now proceeded to count aloud and place six fishes on Nancy's dish, interrupted twice by her demand to substitute a larger specimen.

This accomplished Nancy tendered him a fourpenny bit, but the fishman refused even to look at it.

"Here, gimme fippence," he said roughly.

"I will if you throw another in."

The fishman after a few seconds' deliberation, assuming a heartbroken but resigned expression, threw violently another on the heap.

"Well, on'y it's His Reverence I wouldn't do it," he declared, "for it's just a present of them I'm bestowin' on ye."

"I'm very much obleeged to ye," retorted the victor sarcastically, and returned elated to her kitchen, where Hester was preparing her aunt's midday "arrowroot".

"Professor Ross Jordan's sittin' on the sate. I'm sartin sure the masther'll ask him for dinner, an' what do you think but I got hees in for nothin'."

"We must have a pudding," said Hester excitedly, "is there any milk?"

"Not a skig."

"Then I'll have to make a pie with those windfalls Isaac brought. Do you think will Mr. Shimmens be here too?"

"You bate he will; the masther couldn't well ask one without the other, an' Mr. Shimmens is glued to that sate."

Nancy's prescience proved correct, for on going to announce that dinner was served, the complaisant Mr. Shimmens followed indoors on the professor's heels.

Mrs. Noble expressed great pleasure at seeing the

honoured guest, and regretted that she was unable to hear him preach the day before, as her health incapacitated her for attendance at Divine Service.

Hugh now arrived from Ballyswallow whither he had gone on Saturday for his Sunday's work, and the little difficulty the company experienced in getting wedged in around the small round table, only contributed to Mr. Shimmens's satisfaction, who managed to get as close to Hester as he could.

Nancy stood behind her master's chair until the "blessing" was asked, then removed the dish-cover and withdrew.

"We have here but a few 'small fishes'," quoted the host, helping the professor to what he considered the worthiest on the dish.

"I have read," announced Mr. Shimmens "that the phosphorous contained in fish is beneficial to the brain."

"I'm afraid that's a very fishy story," said Hugh.

"These little fish are always associated with my boyhood's days," said the professor. "I do not believe any other place has conferred so many happy hours on its lovers as Newcastle. The country people used to call it simply 'the salt water'. 'Had you your fortnight yet at "the salt water"?' one friend would ask another."

"Yes, and they applied it internally as well as externally," said Mr. Noble, "for I have often seen them drinking it."

"An old woman," said Hugh, "in my congregation, says that 'time an' again when she was nearly *bate* Newkessel brought her back from the grave.' "

"I remember," said the professor, "a fellow-student of mine who fancied himself an embryo Byron, when staying here once felt urged to compose an ode to the ocean, but all the length he could ever get was the arresting apostrophe 'Stupendous damp'."

"It evidently was enough to 'damp' his muse," remarked Hugh.

"I am sure, Professor," said Mr. Noble, "that you had many warm handshakes yesterday, for you are a *persona grata* in Newcastle."

"Yes, indeed, I had. Several remained to speak to me after the service, but I had a rather ambiguous compliment from my old friend the sexton. Apparently he considered the occasion of not sufficient importance to warrant me being brought such a distance, and this is how he expressed his apology: 'You know, sir, a worse preacher nor you would have done us the day rightly, but we couldn't just lay our hands on him.' "

They laughed as ministers laugh, in a hearty simple way. Indeed, the Rev. Andrew chuckled at intervals during the rest of the meal.

There was more innocent merriment, until the professor looking at his watch arose, and said he was sorry to leave, but a car was waiting to convey him to his sister's in the country.

Hardly had he gone when Oliver appeared. There ensued much lamentation on Mr. Noble's part that the new arrival had missed the great privilege of dining with Professor Ross Jordan. Oliver assured him it would have given him the greatest pleasure. But he looked by no means adequately dejected, as Hester put her hand in his.

Nancy had reserved one of the "small fishes", and Hester was grateful for the little bustle that the cooking of it entailed. For she thought everyone could hear her heart beating, and feared that the rush of colour to her cheeks of which she was so conscious might betray her.

CHAPTER XXVIII

THE PROPOSAL

I give thee all—I can no more
Though poor the offering be.
—KEMBLE.

A FAVOURITE Newcastle social function was a picnic, and on almost the last day of this memorable August, a farewell party was planned in that form; for many of these friends might not meet again until next summer. Then, if still living, you could certainly rely on their appearance on the Newcastle shore in like manner as the swallow is said to return to the same favourite haunts each spring. If, in the meantime, body and soul had parted company, it is almost certain the spirit would return to hover around the dear scenes that soothed it in former days of earthly stress and turmoil.

Slieve Donard was, of course, the goal of the little party. Surely he is the friendliest and most beloved old mountain in the world!—Newcastle's pride and glory—an old coquet that fascinates by unchanging change; seeking to bewitch by surprising variations of expression as sun, wind and rain play hide-and-seek over his wrinkled face. At times he is sulky, and dons his cap and pretends to frighten you, but just wait! there he is beaming with good humour again. Could he but speak, what a revelation of the hearts could he lay bare of those who hailed him friend, of what countless love scenes has he been sole witness! But he is a trusty confidant, for the secrets abide in his heather bosom, and under his grey mists lie hidden all the passions of the human heart.

His ascent is, however, a feat for his favourites, the young—and Mr. Shimmens deserved better treatment at the hands of Hester Temple, seeing that for her sake alone he had undertaken what he considered a superfluous task. His long back was bent, his high cheekbones a dull red, his "kester" he carried in his hand, and the large handkerchief that mopped his perspiring brow lay in it.

On an inviting plateau the ladies spread the welcome tea-table, and any who chose after that might venture higher if so inclined.

It was Mr. Shimmens who first noticed, after having refreshed his inner man with three cups of tea, that Hester had vanished, also that Mr. Whiteside was likewise invisible. A lady who sensed his dismay seized the opportunity for which she had long watched to solace him. It was common knowledge that Miss McMilligan had long been "setting her cap" at the Rev. Obadiah. Indeed, he was thoroughly aware of it himself, even had it not been frequently brought to his notice by the innuendoes to which an unmarried minister has perforce to submit. This lady often averred that spinsterhood was her choice; to retain which state she had required to exert strong will-power. She had been known to confide to a friend that there was not a seat in the demesne on which at some time or other she had not received a proposal. She now attached herself to the forsaken Obadiah and manœuvred him to one of those celebrated seats—for which at least he was thankful—and it may now be said that perseverance received its reward, for Miss McMilligan ended her days in the fine Manse of Tullygig that Hester Temple had disdained.

Meanwhile Hester and Oliver were making a determined and united effort to reach The Cairn, their hands coming into frequent contact as he proffered needless help.

Another pair had strayed in the like direction. "Do you see Hugh and Eunice Gordon?" said Hester. "I do not think it wise of him to pay so much attention to a member of his own congregation, but he always liked a variety. I'm afraid he is not breaking his heart over Eleanor Hill."

"It's more likely she's breaking hers for him," said Oliver, "but when the rich elderly suitor appeared on the scene she could not resist the prospect it offered her."

"And I believe he's an Episcopalian too. I wonder how Dr. Hill swallows that?"

"Oh, the position compensates him too, and there is also talk of Edmund going into the Established Church."

"They were always too snobbish, but Dr. Hill is a really good man. That is *his* weakness. Eunice would suit Hugh better, I think."

But neither of them was to foresee that romance with its painful developments, nor how Hugh—the gay, the debonnair—was to act the Christian chivalrous knight in Eunice's desperate need. That role is not seldom played by the gay-hearted Hughs of the world.

When at last they came to their journey's end a weird feeling overwhelmed the lovers. Here at the great heap of stones they seemed alone in space, on the very top of the world; removed a vast distance from the ordinary earth far below, and as it were in the very Presence of the Creator Himself.

As they rested side by side in that awesome elevation, each felt that to them this moment was predestined; the heavens and earth created for it; Slieve Donard himself upheaved from the abyss, in order to accomplish the fulfilment of their fate.

Said Oliver, "Hester, I have little to offer. Only a love stronger than death. Is that enough?"

Her faint "Yes" flooded his soul with unutterable love and gratitude to the God he worshipped.

"What shall I render unto the Lord for all His benefits?" he involuntarily exclaimed.

"What can we render but our lives," she replied.

....

The short August evening was fast closing in as they turned like Moses to leave the Mount, and like him their faces shone. Hand in hand as they were evermore to go, they turned downwards to the world again. The beauty of twilight softened land and ocean. They turned out of the demesne and went down the steep little hill towards the sea, and as they walked by the wall the great waves dashed themselves against it. It seemed to Hester that even these mad elements shared in the stupendous joy of the moment.

Slowly they wandered through the old world "Promenade", oblivious to other happy lovers seated in obscure nooks. By the fountain played happy children with the unmixed delight of childish abandon that increases as bed-time draws near.

A dark figure was discernible at Pansy Cottage, which resolved itself into that of the Rev. Andrew Noble.

"We feared you had lost your way," he said.

"On the contrary we found it," said Oliver.

They entered the tiny parlour where Mrs. Noble still sat on the sofa refusing to retire until she was assured of the return of the pilgrims. She demanded explanations, which Oliver gladly took it upon himself to deliver.

"Hester has promised to be my wife. I hope Uncle and Aunt you both approve."

Mrs. Noble began to cry softly. Hester sat down beside her and threw her arms around her.

The old minister's eyes moistened, but he said in a firm voice:

"May God's blessing rest upon you both, and may your lives together be as happy as ours have been. Mamma, isn't that what we wish for dear Daughter Hester?"

"Oh! Andrew, you had a poor life with me. Often and often I reproached myself for doing you an injury, by allowing you to marry me."

"Woman! never—never—let such a wicked thought enter your mind again." And the minister declaimed gallantly:

" 'Oh, wert thou in the cauld blast on yonder
    lea, on yonder lea,
My plaidie to the angry airt I'd shelter thee, I'd
    shelter thee.

Or were I monarch of the globe, with thee to
reign, with thee to reign,
The brightest jewel in my crown, wad be my
queen, wad be my queen.'

"What have I to take up now?"

"My shawl and my smelling bottle and my Bible, and oh! I can't find my á Kempis."

"Here he is under the sofa. Now, take my arm up."

. . . .

"I suppose you wouldn't condescend to speak to a poor lonely cousin from the Olympian heights of your happiness."

"Hugh, darling!" Hester ran forward and kissed him. "I hope you will soon be as happy as we are."

The three sat late, not always talking, but with a sense of deep and tender comradeship and understanding.

At length Hester got to her own little room where the breeze from the sea blew inwards the white muslin curtains. How tired she felt! Yet she did not wish to sleep. Through the window all night long came the lullaby of the waves. They sang of love and everlasting joy. Then they changed to a minor key of which the refrain was—"How could you leave Aunt Emily?"

CHAPTER XXIX

THE WEDDING

There was a marriage in Cana of Galilee
.... and Jesus was called.
—JOHN ii. I.

ON a day of the following April when sun and rain alternated, as laughter and tears are wont to do at the merriest bridal, Oliver and Hester were married.

The wedding was actually facilitated by Aunt Emily, who, when Hester suggested that she felt it her duty to stay with her, rose to the crisis, and showed forth her genuine Christianity which surmounted the trying test.

"Dear," said Aunt Emily, "you must not dream of such a thing. I have thought it all over, and I'm certain Lucy Marshall would be glad to come. She has no home of her own, poor thing! and she has been often here and knows the ways of the house. But, of course, dear Hester, she will never be to your uncle and me what you have been. I shall be all the happier sitting here, for knowing that you are happy, although far away." She drew Hester's head down—"Dear, I am glad it wasn't Mr. Shimmens."

On the morning of that most portentous day of her life Hester awoke early to the singing of the birds, and lay still thinking. Was it joy or sorrow she felt? She could scarcely tell, for rarely does one come without bringing the other in its train. Of one thing she was supremely certain, the guidance of that Unseen Hand that had led her hitherto; and on her knees she committed her whole future into Its safe keeping.

She found Nancy making the porridge, for nothing short of a cyclone would interrupt that almost sacred rite with which her master and mistress's day began and ended.

Nancy was plainly excited. "Did you smell them? I'm afeard they're a wee bit swinged, for I'm that throughother I forgot to stir them. I'm just turnin' roun' an' roun' an' can get no forrader."

There was a heavy step on the stairs.

"Well, if there's not the masther himself, an' the table not even set. Wet you the tay an' put on the saucepan for the eggs while I set about it."

When all was ready, Hester as always carried up her aunt's tray, propped her up in bed, and wrapped a warm shawl round her.

"Please hand me a clean handkerchief out of the drawer," and Hester having done so, went to the window while her aunt wiped her eyes.

"Is it going to be a nice day?"

"Beautiful," said Hester.

Mrs. Noble searched under her pillow, and put a small box in Hester's hand. "With my dearest love," she said.

"Dear Aunt Emily, how can I thank you?" In Hester's hand lay a little old square gold brooch set around with pearls, her aunt's greatest treasure.

Words rose to Hester's lips, but she could not utter them. How she yearned to thank this Mother-Aunt for the years that lay behind! Never had she grudged her anything. Indeed in the matter of adornment, she had often failed to satisfy her aunt's requirements; for a life of semi-invalidism had not deprived Aunt Emily of a love of dress. Under her shawls was always a silk dress, and at either side of her face, beneath the black lace of her cap, dangled a curl.

"Dear Aunt Emily, I wasn't half good enough to you!" She kissed her aunt's wet cheek and fled.

Breakfast proved an even worse ordeal. Her uncle kept gazing steadily out of the window as if some interesting manœuvres were being carried out on the lawn. Hester, who had always sat facing it and knew every bush and tree by heart, looked at them this morning with new affection, as at dear old friends one leaves behind.

Lucy Marshall, who had come to take her place, and was to be her bridesmaid, ate steadily on.

Lastly, Hugh appeared, carrying that spirit of nonchalance that relieves tense situations, declared his tea "dish-water", and said he might at least have had a respectable cup of tea on his wedding day.

"Hugh," reproved his father, "this day should be begun in seriousness."

"I am entirely serious about the tea," affirmed Hugh.

Nancy entered with a pair of boots in her hand. "You should have got a new pair, sir," she said, addressing her master, "it's not fit for you to go to a weddin' with shoes cut to aise your corns."

"Nancy, as always, is traditionally correct," said Hugh, "to feel comfortable at a wedding is outrageous."

The minister rose. "As soon as you are ready, Hugh, we'll have Worship."

It was Mr. Noble's custom to read a chapter in strict succession throughout the Bible. This morning it happened to be that of 1st Chronicles which records the unpronounceable, if honoured names, of those who performed in David's choir. The minister who would have gone to the stake rather than endure an instrument in public worship grappled conscientiously with the fourteen sons and three daughters of Heman who "helped to lift up the horn". Had anyone "helped to lift up the horn" in Taraghan Meeting-house, the Rev. Andrew Noble would have thought that Satan had been let loose in that pure Zion. Hester, however, was grateful to these "sons and daughters of Heman", for their outlandish names touched no tender chords in her heart. But as she knelt she dreaded her uncle's prayer.

It began as of other mornings, confession of unworthiness, intercession for Sabbath breakers and other evildoers. Even the followers of the "false prophet" were not overlooked. "And now our Heavenly Father," the tone of the voice grew very tender, "we pray Thee specially for the beloved one who goes forth from our midst to-day. God bless her!" His fluency vanished ... "we give her into Thy guardianship for this world and that which is to come..."

Hester did not hear the end, but felt it was abrupt. When she braced herself to turn round, she found herself alone with her aunt.

After putting the finishing touches to the simple lunch, which would wait them after the ceremony, the young bride dressed, and when ready to go came to show herself to Mrs. Noble.

"Walk over to the window," commanded her aunt. And after thoughtful scrutiny, she said, "I was right about the third flounce, although it did take more silk. Pull your bonnet just a little farther forward, now draw your veil across."

Hester obeyed and the white Limerick lace fell like a curtain over face and neck.

"You do look very genteel (it was the adjective of the day) I knew that dark blue check silk would make up elegantly over the crinoline."

"It was all your good choice, Aunt Emily, and I'm glad to do you credit."

Hester holding in her hand a tight little posy sent by Lady Dingle, of white camellias and myrtle set in a stiff paper frill, stepped into the carriage which had brought Oliver from Newcastle, where he had stayed the previous night. Lucy followed, but Nancy refused to come inside. She had often seen Lady Dingle's maid on the box beside the coachman. She would also keep up the dignity of *her* family, and let the people see she "knew her place".

Isaac in his Sunday-go-to-meetin' garments was standing at the church gate when they arrived, but affected not to notice them. He deigned, however, to inspect the carriage horses before shuffling into a back pew.

Hester walked up the aisle on Hugh's arm, and had a vague notion she was standing beside Oliver. She saw as in a dream her uncle take up a Bible and proceed to find the place, but something was amiss—he had forgotten to put on his spectacles! She anxiously followed his search through various pockets. At length they were forthcoming. This little incident braced both minister and bride. At times his voice betrayed him, but the prayers in the presence of the congregation were less trying than those in the close home circle.

It was over! Her uncle kissed her, and Lucy kissed her, and Hugh. As she walked down the aisle—a winsome happy bride, old friends on every side smiled their good-byes. Thus she passed in love and affection from the old Meeting-house, in whose Sabbath School she had been both teacher and taught, where she had taken her first Communion, and within whose walls she had drawn Sabbath by Sabbath very nigh her Lord and Saviour.

Her hand rested in her husband's on the drive home. It seemed as solemn a part of the day as the Service.

At the open door stood Nancy, still in the glory of her red bonnet, her Paisley shawl exchanged for a grand new white apron.

Mrs. Noble sat on the drawing-room sofa in her best silk dress and point lace collar. Round her shoulders was a much-prized Indian shawl that had made a considerable hole in Hugh's first stipend. She came into the parlour on her son's arm, sat at the table supported by cushions, and received without protest a wing of chicken on her plate.

There was another pretence at eating. Hugh affected to be particularly merry. "I wanted to cry," said Lucy Marshall, "when uncle pronounced you man and wife, but when I put my hand in my pocket I had forgotten my handkerchief, so that frightened me out of it."

Fortunately there was little time on hand. Hester and Lucy disappeared upstairs. The bride returned in a long brown pelisse and brown drawn silk travelling bonnet. She clung a little to her aunt. There were embraces, tears, and blessings. And Hester Whiteside passed between the white lilacs and golden laburnums, out of the gates of the safe old homestead, her heart wholly trusting in her husband and her husband's God.

GLOSSARY

The definitions in the following glossary are for the most part taken from William Hugh Patterson's *A Glossary of Words and Phrases used in Antrim and Down* (1880) and James Fenton's *The Hamely Tongue: A Personal Record of Ulster-Scots in County Antrim* (4th edition, 2014).

afeard	*frightened*
afore	*before*
agin	*against*
apern	*apron*
atween	*between*
aye	*always*
aye (2)	*yes*
baird	*beard*
bat	*blow (strike)*
bate	*beat*
bees	*is*
beetle	*a pestle-like pounder*
blackavised	*dark-complexioned*
blackmouth	*Presbyterian (contempt.)*
blate	*bashful*
blether-come-skite	*someone who talks nonsense*
blethers	*rambling nonsense talk*

body	*person*
brave	*fine, large*
brownkaties	*bronchitis*
champ	*(v) mash*
chew	*command to a dog to be quiet*
clabber	*soft mud*
clane	*clean*
clash	*gossip*
clockin'	*hatching*
comether	*come hither*
cowp	*overturn*
crack	*chat*
crack (2)	*moment*
cranch	*crunch*
cranoge	*man-made island in a river or lake*
crayther	*creature*
crulged	*crouched, stooped*
dale	*deal*
dandher	*leisurely walk*
day-le-gone	*dusk*
deef	*deaf*
dickey	*driver's seat on a carriage*
divarshun	*diversion, entertainment*

doncy	*sickly*
dooless	*useless, worthless*
dunch	*nudge*
dwam	*weakness, fainting fit*
farls	*quarter segments of flat griddle bread*
fash	*trouble oneself*
flype	*(prob.) shred*
forbye	*besides*
forrad	*forward*
foundher	*(n) a cold*
ganched	*stammered, stuttered*
geb	*chatter*
girnin	*complaining*
gomerils	*fools*
gomish	*blockhead*
gumption	*common sense*
gunk	*shock*
heartscald	*persistent nuisance or worry*
hirplin'	*limping*
hussy	*girl*
indeed an' doubles	*indeed (with added emphasis)*
juke	*duck the head*
kale	*cabbage*

kennel	*candle*
kester	*(castor) top hat*
kettle	*cattle*
latther end	*end*
lief lone	*absolutely alone*
lip	*taste, sample*
loanen	*lane*
lock	*a quantity*
meat	*food*
Methody	*Methodist*
mind	*remember*
mind (2)	*remind*
moiley	*hornless cow*
narra'	*narrow, tightfisted*
near-han'	*near*
nebbity	*big nosed*
newens	*a novelty*
nor	*than*
not tear in the pluckin'	*wouldn't be of tender years*
notionate	*obstinate*
outbye	*outdoors*
oxthercog	*support under the arms*
pechin'	*panting*
pickle next the wind	*next in line to be married*

pig-crue	*pig sty*
pirdas	*potatoes*
puttin' spake on	*(prob.) bespeaking, laying claim in advance to*
quare / quare an'	*very*
quarest	*strangest*
rared	*raised*
redd up	*tidy up*
ree	*fresh, lively, frisky*
scouldin'	*telling off*
scuffled	*raked or hoed lightly*
scunner	*(n) an aversion*
shough	*ditch*
shutes	*suits*
sitherwood	*southernwood*
skelly	*squintiness*
skellied	*squinty-eyed*
skig	*drop*
sonsy	*comely*
sprickley-begs	*sticklebacks*
steepins	*stipends*
stirabout	*porridge*
stoor / stour	*dust, disturbance*
stravagin	*wandering, roaming*

suddint	*sudden*
swally	*swallow*
swarree	*soirée*
swinge	*singe*
(in) swithers	*wavering, undecided*
syne	*afterwards, then*
tay	*tea*
teem	*pour*
the day	*today*
thole	*bear, endure*
thon	*that*
thonder	*yonder*
thrawin	*awkward, recalcitrant*
throng	*busy*
throughother	*confused, untidy*
toul'	*told*
true blue	*Presbyterian*
weans	*children*
wersh	*bitter or rancid*
whack	*share*
wheen	*a quantity, number*
widda	*widow*
windy	*window*

10033126R00141

Printed in Great Britain
by Amazon.co.uk, Ltd.,
Marston Gate.